NOSEDIVE INTO HELL!

I'll die here, Islaen thought even as she dove for the floor, instinctively clutching Bandit to her so that her body might serve as a shield for the little Jadite.

There was a vast shuddering, then a bounce followed by two others. Intense heat and fire followed fast, filling all the air above her. Her hair was singeing—she could smell it. She could smell burning flesh as well, strongly enough that she gagged on the reek, but that was not hers. The exposed skin of her neck was blistering, but other than that, she was as yet untouched . . .

She had to get out, get the others out!

STAR COMMANDOS

JUNGLE ASSAULT

P.M. GRIFFIN

ACE BOOKS, NEW YORK

STAR COMMANDOS: JUNGLE ASSAULT

An Ace Book / published by arrangement with
the author

PRINTING HISTORY
Ace edition / April 1991

ISBN: 0-441-78335-X

Ace Books are published by The Berkley Publishing Group,
200 Madison Avenue, New York, New York 10016.
The name "ACE" and the "A" logo
are trademarks belonging to Charter Communications, Inc.

PRINTED IN THE UNITED STATES OF AMERICA

10 9 8 7 6 5 4 3 2 1

To my friend,
Maria DiPaola.

ONE

COMMANDO-COLONEL ISLAEN Connor rested her head against the wall and closed her eyes for a moment, trying to banish her discomfort. Amazoon of Indra was plaguey hot even here at the supposedly temperate poles.

She roused herself to glance at her companions and saw with perverse gratification that they were no more content than she. None of them was making a display of the fact, but she knew them all well, and it required no exercise of her ability to detect the emotions of those around her in order to realize that this unrelenting heat and humidity did not make them happy.

Sitting close beside her to her right, his dark eyes shut, was Commando-Captain Varn Tarl Sogan. Once a war prince and Admiral of the Arcturian Empire and commander of the invasion fleet she had battled on Thorne of Brandine during the final years of the War, he was now second to her in the elite guerrilla unit she led and her husband, or her consort, as he would have said.

A little apart from them was her long-time comrade and fellow Noreenan, Commando-Captain Jake Karmikel. Despite the temperature, the redhead's arm was casually draped around his deceptively diminutive companion—though no one who knew the space-bred Commando-Sergeant Bethe Danlo doubted either her toughness or her right to a place in this company.

Islaen smiled sympathetically. The pair had just spent the tail end of their honeymoon trying to outguess and combat a volcano, and if their information was accurate, they were soon

1

to pit themselves against an unknown number of either pirates or the subbiotics who dealt with them.

Her head shook imperceptibly. She and Varn had passed their marriage furlough in battle for Astarte's life against a full pirate armada, and they had seen little in the way of peace since. Trouble came with a Commando's uniform, and it seemed to ride all her team with particular force.

Collecting stardust, Colonel?

She glanced at the former Admiral as his thought touched hers. They had discovered during their first days together, on Visnu of Brahmin, that they could converse mind with mind, an ability they took great care to conceal from all but these close comrades here with them, even as they guarded the other, differing gifts of the mutations that had touched them and set them apart from the remainder of their species.

Just trying to keep even my mind from working too hard in this heat.

Yes! Amazoon's not nice!

Her expression softened as she looked down at the tiny creature perched on her knee, plumage extended to the full to afford her maximum cooling. Bandit was without question the strangest member of this or any other team in all the Federation. The Jadite gurry looked to be no more than a particularly appealing mascot, a seven-ounce bundle of brown feathers relieved by a thin black stripe circling her head, covering the merry black eyes like the mask of a pre-space Terran robber. The broad, bright yellow bill was supple enough to give further expression to her face, and the equally vivid legs sported toes as useful as any human's hand.

Cute, she was, but the little hen, along with the rest of her kind, possessed both the power of decision and the ability to communicate in mind not only with others of her own species but with those humans with whom she was bonded. Beyond that, she consciously radiated large volumes of goodwill, influencing nearly any sentient being not utterly depraved or in the grip of exceptionally violent emotion to favor both herself and her companions. These gifts, too, her human comrades kept in close secret for her protection and the protection of all her species and her homeworld, Jade of Kuan Yin.

Sogan reached over to scratch her head. *Patience, small one. We will soon be airborne.* He glanced at his auburn-haired commander. *Am I assuming too much in believing our hosts probably do climate control their transports?*

She frowned slightly. *They're not trying to prove anything with us, Varn. It's just that this is their winter, and they really do find it comfortably cool.*

I know, he apologized quickly. *I guess I was remembering Thorne too fondly.*

Her eyes sparkled. *Thorne's nippy, my space-spoiled friend. I think you were dreaming of the* Fairest Maid *and the ideal temperatures you program for her.*

Spoiled? I am not the one who finds our adopted homeworld a might brisk at times, he replied, unruffled. *However, my question does stand. Do you think we will be riding in reasonable comfort or putting up with more of this?*

The former, most likely. Amazoonans use their vehicles planet-wide, over and in all her jungles. Even the northern-most areas where we'll be going are plenty hot and muggy enough to warrant cooling.

Karmikel glowered at them. "Listen, you three. Mind talk may be fine in its place, but if you're going to chatter away in our company, how about including Bethe and me?"

"Sorry, Jake," Islaen responded contritely. "It comes so naturally now that I really do forget about verbal speech at times. —We weren't saying much, just talking about the heat."

He made a wry face. "It's worth mentioning, all right," he grumbled. "We do seem to wind up on some of the ultrasystem's wonder spots, don't we?"

"Travel is part of the job, Comrade."

"What if we get to target only to find it's got nothing to do with the Alpha Gary arms?"

"That's not beyond the realm of possibility," the Colonel admitted. Her voice turned grim. "No matter. We'll take care of it anyway. Whatever's going on here is nasty. Innocents and minor crooks don't pass their time shooting people out of the sky."

A few weeks previously, a shipment of Navy armaments had vanished from the docks on Alpha Gary in a brazen and obviously well-planned theft that had sent both the military and the Stellar Patrol into a near panic. The potential for disaster was awesome should that matériel fall into the hands of a pirate fleet or would-be surplanetary conqueror or dictator, and no effort was being spared to locate the shipment and those who had taken it. Her company's mission to Tambora of Pele had been in search of it. They had found no connection, although they had encountered trouble in plenty. Now, they had been sent to Amazoon of Indra on the same hunt.

Apparently, there was greater reason to believe they were navigating in the correct starlane this time. Less than a week previously, the Amazoonan government had contacted Intelligence with the report of an incident that, because of the timing and the jungle world's location, seemed a good enough indication that what they sought might be here that the Navy's best troubleshooting unit had been ordered to investigate on all burners—and to retake or destroy the arms should they indeed be concealed here.

Chance had revealed the clue. The raw courage and determination of one woman had brought it to light.

While on a normal high-altitude patrol, a Yeoman of the surplanetary military, the Jungle Rangers, had spotted a glinting in one of the rare clearings in the treelands far below and had descended to investigate. As she neared canopy level, a missile had suddenly slammed into her flier.

The gunner's aim had been somewhat off, enough so that the craft spun out of control and crashed in the treetops instead of detonating immediately in midair. The bleeding pilot had just time to scramble out of it before it transformed itself into a ball of all-consuming flame.

She had realized full well that she had no hope of rescue before her wounds and the jungle killed her, not if she waited where she was, even assuming she could avoid those who had brought her down. Sorely injured as she was, she had drawn on all her knowledge of her homeworld, all the skill her years with the Rangers had given her, and had walked out, making her way alone and afoot through the treelands and over the Barrier Ridge all the distance to the settled lands of the Far North. Every one of the numerous lacerations scoring her body was infected, and she had suffered the agonies of Amazoon's steaming hell from leeches and insects, but she had survived and had brought with her the report of what she had seen and what had happened to her.

The Yeoman's actual observations were scant enough in themselves. She had glimpsed three ships, starships, she believed medium-sized freighters of about a ten-man class. That discovery under other circumstances would hardly have amazed either her or her superiors. Smugglers did occasionally utilize, or try to utilize, Amazoon's jungles for the cover they afforded, and those seeking to rape her of her priceless hardwoods were an ever-looming menace. Constant watching and patrolling were necessary to combat both. It was the missile that gave everyone pause. None of those the Rangers normally encountered would have possessed a weapon of that power, and few would have dared use it, realizing full well the response its firing would elicit from on-world and Federation officials alike once the incident became known. That these intruders did have it and had felt compelled to use it was stark testimony to the magnitude of their purpose and their determination to prevent any premature revelation or disruption of their plans. Equally frightening was their readiness to spend so potent a weapon on one small flier. They almost certainly had another, and probably several others, at their disposal. That was what had made the Amazoonan government call in the Navy and what had drawn such immediate response.

"Letting off that missile was a mite unfriendly," the Noreenan man agreed with his commander. "Not to mention a bit stupid."

"Not really," Bethe Danlo interjected. "They doubtless believed they'd wipe out the scout in one shot and that no one'd discover what'd happened to her, at least not until after they were long gone."

Islaen nodded. "Bethe's reading it right, I think. Who'd imagine anyone would walk away from the kind of wreck that Yeoman described, much less make her way out of those treelands without supplies or transport of any kind? Her planet's gods and fortune were with her in a high degree, and folks just don't take those into much consideration in real life." She shook her head. "No, our trigger-happy friends won't be much concerned on her account." Her tone became sharper. "The incident won't cause them to light their burners any faster, but we still have to worry that they'll finish up and vanish into space again before we have a chance to get to them."

There was no need to stress that possibility. Amazoon's treelands were not hospitable to off-worlders. The thick canopy and lack of population provided excellent cover and security for a time, but the jungle inevitably took its toll. Crew members soon sickened if their shots had not been specifically augmented to meet the challenges of the planet. Cargoes deteriorated. Even armaments not specifically prepared and treated for this environment all too quickly began to suffer from exposure to it.

Her eyes flickered to the door of the small office where they were waiting. It led to the cavernous, bustling expanse of the Rangers' main transport hangar, and she could feel a change in the transmissions of those working near them, a rise in excitement and tension. The preparations were over or just about over. They would be leaving shortly. Whether anything was left for them to discover or fight, that remained to be seen.

TWO

A FAMILIAR MIND pattern approached the entrance. "Get set," Islaen told the others even as she called out in reply to the anticipated knock.

The man who responded was strikingly tall, as were all his race, and proportionally well built, neither thin nor overmuscled. His broad features were handsome according to the general southern Terran prototype, his hair and eyes very dark in keeping with his complexion.

"Ready to face the jungle, Commandos?"

"As ready as you are, Sergeant," Islaen Connor replied, coming lightly to her feet, "figuratively speaking, that is. I doubt any off-worlders want much to do with it in-depth."

Varn Tarl Sogan silently echoed that last statement as they followed their guide into the hangar. He suspected that Simon Salombo did as well if there was any truth at all in the reports he had read of Amazoon and her inhabitants while en route to the green planet. These Jungle Rangers were a tough crew and capable of meeting the challenges set by their harsh homeworld as no others could do, but they were neither fools nor shooting stars. Danger and hardship were to be endured and overcome in need. They were never to be courted.

Bethe sighed to herself. Jake Karmikel was a big man, and even he seemed undersized beside these Amazoonans. She looked and, worse, felt like a child when near them. Would she have trouble because of that, apart from the sense of inadequacy it gave her? Too many people tended to judge competence by size . . .

The former Admiral seemed to recognize her discomfort, or

perhaps shared it. He gave her a quick, encouraging smile before turning his attention to the thick-bodied troop carrier that was to bring them to their target.

He studied it carefully without seeming to do so. The vehicle was well maintained but it was nothing out of the ordinary, just another large, enclosed airborne transport whose like could be found on countless colony and agrarian worlds throughout the Federation ultrasystem fulfilling a variety of heavy-duty chores whose number was limited only by the imagination and ingenuity of those using them.

So it was here. This particular craft was outfitted to carry personnel and their gear. Others berthed nearby obviously hefted heavy or bulky cargo, and a few handled more specialized chores. Two that he noted seemed to be designed for research work, to carry out detailed studies at different altitudes. One might be used for rescue work, and he thought a fourth was a fire fighter, rare as major conflagrations would be in Amazoon of Indras ever-wet treelands.

The off-worlders and their escort reached the transport in a couple of minutes. Salombo ushered them aboard through the tail hatch. "We've given you the rear seats," he explained in a deep-voiced, musically rhythmic Basic pleasant to hear. "You'll get the best view there. We'll be going in low to avoid high-altitude scanners, and the canopy's worth seeing at that level. So's the Barrier Ridge. Even our veterans give that more than a passing glance every time they fly over."

They would also be spared the need to walk the length of the craft and the inevitable inspection by those they passed. A considerate gesture, Islaen thought. "How many are in your party, Sergeant?"

"Thirty plus our pilot and me. We'll get you there and give you whatever support you need or want. —We're completely under your orders as far as the approach and assault go. You need have no fear about that, Colonel Connor."

"I don't," she answered him quietly. "I like what I see of your people. I'd be more concerned about trying to work with some Regular units than with you Jungle Rangers." She smiled suddenly. "I only hope we can keep up with you when we have to go it on foot."

He flashed her a wide smile in return. "No problem. We'll move real slow." The Amazoonan grew serious. "There's no avoiding that part of it, unfortunately. We'd have no more luck than my Yeoman if we tried to go in all the way by air."

"We appreciate that fact."

"It won't be easy," he warned. "It's leech country that we'll be crossing, not the worst in the jungle perhaps, but you can put credits down that there'll be quite a few of the little beggars around, and nowhere's free of bugs, not even the middle of the big rivers."

"The actual walking won't be that bad, though, will it?"

"No. The canopy doesn't give undergrowth much of a chance. The big tangles're along the waterways or where one of the trees came down for one reason or another. You won't find that near target. The intruders have considerably burned out the vegetation in the clearing for us."

He fell silent after that. The transport had begun to roll toward the yawning mouth of the hangar, and everyone was preparing for takeoff. The Commando-Colonel hastened to claim her seat, that by the window. Varn slid in next to her, then the on-world Sergeant. Jake and Bethe Danlo already occupied the two seats across the aisle from them. Theirs was a double rather than a triple row, and so they did not share a place with any of the Amazoonans.

She could see the dark heads of her fellow passengers straighten in front of her as their craft nosed toward the daylight.

The transport glided through the door, maneuvering with a seemingly effortless ease that belied its somewhat clumsy appearance, and taxied a surprisingly short distance down the almost maddeningly straight runway before a gentle bump informed those within that they were in the air.

They climbed steadily for several minutes, then leveled off. At that point, Islaen and those around her visibly relaxed.

The Noreenan woman smiled to herself. That instinctive stiffening upon rising and landing was probably as old as mechanical flight itself.

She forgot her companions then as her eyes fixed on the world below. It was an orderly, pleasant scene, doubly attractive to one of her agrarian background. There was variety in plenty. Tall, closely massed, dark green growth made up the bulk of the landscape, tree farms of one sort or another. Amazoon's hardwoods were famous throughout the ultrasystem both for their utility and their beauty, and many of her fruits and nuts enjoyed a steady if less spectacular market. Lower patches and what looked like open fields from this altitude supported tuber-producing plants and those involved in the planet's enormous medicinal industry. Pools and canals of every size and form contained fish and other water life, while the seemingly utterly wild tangle of low brush and vines lining their banks were actually capa pastures.

The dwellings and outbuildings of every three or four farms were clustered together, but no larger communities presented themselves to her sight, nor were there many such anywhere on the planet. High-quality surplanetary communications and transportation rendered gross population density unnecessary for maintaining unity, and Amazoon's denizens were as adamant as those of her own Noreen about keeping the impact of their presence as low as was conceivably possible while still supporting the growth of individuals and the society they formed.

With the suddenness of a blow, of the fall of an axe, the human-induced order ceased to exist. In one place were Amazoon's prosperous farms. In the next, as if parted by a carefully drawn line, rose the lush canopy of a primeval jungle.

Simon Salombo had been watching for her reaction and was gratified to see her start of surprise. "The halting of our expansion is as intentional as it appears," he told her proudly. "My ancestors knew what they had when they claimed Amazoon of Indra. They knew what her trees were worth even then, but they realized, too, how fragile an ecosystem like this really is, how few generations of abuse would be required to reduce this world to a husk capable only of supporting a few imported beasts and crops.

"It was a hard way, and a lot of people called us fools at the time, but we decided to work with our planet, to take nothing we did not replace and to maintain the greater part of her in trust rather than merely as a gift of some god that was ours to squander without thought or feeling.

"We colonized only the poles, chiefly this one since there's very little land at the South, and we've confined ourselves strictly to the area originally designated for our use by those who first shipped here. By the same token, of course, we've held our population tightly in control, never exceeding the

level set by them, a number just sufficient to maintain us as a
healthy and viable race."

His head raised. "We farm our trees and harvest our fruits
and tubers, milk our capas, fish our lakes and rivers. We
manufacture medicines used by the whole Federation and
constantly work to discover and develop more. In the process,
we've become one of the most prosperous peoples per capita in
the ultrasystem. Don't let the simplicity of our life-style fool
you. Our pleasures may be quieter and more individual-
oriented than those of an urban civilization, but our homes
equal any on Hedon short of a merchant prince's palace for
comfort and convenience. Our culture is rich, with roots
extending far back into Terra's ancient past."

The woman nodded. That, she had very quickly come to
recognize. Amazoonan visual arts were too far removed from
the standards of her own race for her to appreciate them on
more than an intellectual level, but their music was another
matter. There was a power and a force to it, a raw beauty that
drew her strongly enough that she was bringing several
recordings away with her for her pleasure and Varn's on the
Fairest Maid and in their headquarters on Thorne of Brandine.

Her respect and liking for this people did not blunt the
Colonel's awareness of the less creditable penchants of her
species. "An admirable goal and one you're to be congratu-
lated for maintaining and achieving as you have, but it can't
always have been an easy struggle to hold to it."

The big man shrugged. "As I said, our ancestors worked,
and we work still. As for the rest, the Jungle Rangers were
formed in chief to manage those who don't care for the way
we've chosen to use our planet and her resources. The Green
Lady knows, there's always been enough of that detritus
roaming the starlanes."

"And your jungles as well, unless your race has somehow
performed a genetic miracle and exempted itself from greed."

"Hardly," Simon said. "We have our share of vermin. They
just spread their rot in other ways and don't trouble the wild
lands or the areas under cultivation, either. Those're the prime
concerns of we Rangers."

He anticipated her skepticism, although she was too practiced at schooling her responses for him to actually read it.
"One man went after the trees, only one, many, many

generations ago. Because his crime was an attack on the planet herself, a threat of ultimate destruction of the life forms to which she had given rise and which she nurtured, not merely a violation of the laws we colonists had made, he was tried for treason." The Sergeant's face became cold and as hard as titanone. "Upon his conviction, he was given maximum sentence and turned over to Amazoon of Indra for execution."

Islaen frowned, concealing the chill she felt grip her. "What do you mean?"

"He was stripped and bound fast in a leech grove and left there."

Salombo shrugged. "He died fast enough. More importantly, that sentence remains on the books for what he tried to do, and the determination to invoke it remains in our people. That has been sufficient to deter any more of my people from putting themselves in danger of meeting such a death."

The Noreenan eyed him somberly. "It wouldn't have stopped some of the vermin spawned by any other race, Simon Salombo, not with the kind of profits a cargo of Amazoonan timber could bring even on the black market. Your folk're no plasma spines. I can't believe that none of those lacking a conscience would fail to make the dare."

There was no humor in his answering smile. "True enough, Colonel, but you're forgetting how really tightly we control the export of our woods, finished or raw. It would be very easy to trace any piece of it surfacing off-world—and everyone connected with it. As I told you, the penalty for raping Amazoon's wild is well known, and it wouldn't be waived. That's known, too. We may not be plasma spines, but we're not utter fools, either."

Varn Tarl Sogan listened to the Colonel's exchange with Salombo but took no part in it. In his own mind, he agreed with the man's and his people's reasoning. Arcturian law was hard as well, with little scope for leniency even for minor offenders, and it was rare when any of his race had to feel its wrath. They appreciated its power and the inevitability of its lash too well. He had known what lay before him when he refused to destroy Thorne of Brandine at the War's end . . .

He looked beyond Islaen, fixed his eyes on the window and on that part of the world below that was visible to him.

It was an awesome sight even from this altitude, and it was beautiful, at least in the face the canopy presented to him. He could see vivid patches of color amid the ocean of deep green. Some trees were always in flower in the jungle, glowing with orange or pink, blue as clear as Thorne's sky, white, yellow that was like solid sunlight. There were fruits as well, on trees whose flowers were spent, though those were invisible from here. He and his comrades had sampled some of their produce since their arrival on-world and had found most rich and sweet, a delight for human and gurry alike. The rest were pleasantly tart.

None of that comforted him. He felt too keenly that this was a surface fairness, a surface friendliness, that what lay in the heart of this vast wilderness was something very different, a spirit entirely inimical to all his kind.

Of a certainty, that canopy was a great deal more than it seemed in this quick glance. It was home to the bulk of the planet's life. Those great crowns supported vines and seedlings of every sort plus an uncounted and nearly uncountable variety of epiphytes, each basking in its own preferred level of light from full sun to a well-filtered glow at the lowest branches.

Those plants, in turn, gave refuge and food to animals, many in symbiotic relationships with a single genus or even a single species. There were tiny ants and flying insects that nested within leaves and stems, larger creatures that fed upon the vegetation. Amphibians grew to maturity and swam and mated as adults in rainwater pools caught in cupped leaves and flowers or in indented places on branches. Birds nested and sought their food among the leaves in seemingly infinite variety and size, from minute nectar sippers smaller than a man's thumb to large raptors well able to take all but the largest reptile and mammalian denizens of that high world for their prey.

Of the mammals, a very great part of them were rodents. The order was immensely successful on Amazoon of Indra, and its members had adapted to fill every conceivable niche provided in their rich environment, including those occupied on many other worlds by the nearly absent primates. Most were vegetarians in this world so superbly suited to meet a plant-eater's needs, but there were predators in plenty as well, warm- and cold-blooded both, fast, agile, and lithe, well fitted for their work of keeping their prey's numbers in check and their populations strong and viable.

None of this troubled the war prince, although he knew that several of the hunters were either large enough to threaten a lone man or else possessed highly toxic venoms. Nearly all of those were exclusively dwellers of the canopy and rarely if ever voluntarily ventured to the jungle floor where humans might encounter them.

He did not shrink from the place merely because it was wild. The sea—any water—he loved. He liked mountains and high country, and he liked forests such as they had encountered on Anath of Algola. The jungle was something different. It was an alien world inimical to human life. That generations of people had existed and flourished from time immemorial in such environments on countless planets throughout the Federation ultrasystem was no reassurance. That green realm down there remained an enemy in his eyes, actively hostile and stronger than any strength he could hope to set against it. He did not look forward to the time they would have to spend within its grasp, however strong, well-supplied, and wise in its ways their party might be.

Sogan knew what to expect. The tapes he had studied had told him that. There was no brightness, no flood of Indra's golden light down there. All was dim and perpetually shadowed far beneath the canopy, and it was unceasingly damp. Humidity was a constant 90 degrees or more, and some rain fell nearly every day, with sprays and droplets continuing to seep through and drip from the thick overhead cover long after the clouds had ceased to release their store of moisture. Temperatures remained in the high 80's even at this latitude and time of year.

The soil was thin and poor, for decomposition was quick, and the great trees took back almost immediately whatever they put into it in the form of fallen leaves or fruit. That poverty plus the dim, diffused light reaching the ground kept it all but clear of undergrowth. Only in the open places by the numerous watercourses and in the clearings formed by the fall of one of the forest giants, which usually took down at least the interlocking branches of its neighbors as well, did saplings and shrub growth run rampant. Such areas, aptly titled tangles, were difficult and at times impossible to breach if they extended any distance inland.

Beyond these patches of lesser and younger plants, for mile after endless mile, the hardwoods reigned. Their height and growth patterns varied in response to local conditions. Those in this region, as throughout most of the planet, rose almost branchless to mushroom-shaped crowns three to four hundred feet above the jungle floor.

The trees were closely set for their size, and nearly all of them were braced by massive buttresses that sometimes extended as much as forty feet out from their parent trunks so that some climbing and clambering on the part of travelers was necessary despite the lack of secondary growth. A number of species sported great aerial roots as well that worked their way downward until they reached the soil and then thickened into secondary trunks as they penetrated and fed from it until a composite tree of vast circumstances was formed. Old specimens could measure one hundred or more feet in diameter.

Vines were everywhere, some thin as pencils, some like strong, young saplings in their own right. They climbed along their supports until they broke through the canopy only to descend again to rest in the thin soil and begin the long ascent once more.

Such country quickly disabled the sense of direction. Effective visibility extended only a few feet, and sound carried little farther. Even most signaling gear was muted here. Only powerful communications devices could project past the thick canopy to reach craft ranging overhead, much less a transceiver any distance away. Given those conditions, his admiration for the Ranger Yeoman grew stronger each time he recalled her feat in walking out of that hellish trap. It would have been an awesome deed had she been whole, and she had been injured, severely so . . .

The Arcturian shook his head. She had had to contend with wildlife as well as terrain. Very few creatures of any size inhabited the treeland floor save near the good browse and subsequent fine hunting in and around the tangles, and with care, one could avoid them fairly readily. Greater caution was needed to prevent unpleasant encounters with smaller, venom-bearing beasts both in the more open jungle and in the overgrown places, but none of those were the real terror of Amazoon of Indra, or of any jungle region for that matter.

The giantism rampant at the planet's equator—typified by the forty-foot slugs Islaen Connor had once mentioned—was not to be found in these higher latitudes, but insects and other pests abounded, and sometimes it was the smallest that proved the greatest plagues. Amazoon's many leeches were the most repulsive of these defenders of the wild, but in truth, her ants and stinging and biting flies were as bad or worse, albeit their assaults were rarely life-threatening. Thanks to the immunization shots they had received, there was nothing to fear from the diseases of which they might otherwise have been the victims.

Rivers provided the best and most convenient roads for surface travel, but they were far from ideal highways. They were all characterized by fast, rough stretches and drops and waterfalls of every size. Powerful, unpredictable currents were a potentially deadly hazard for small craft, as was large-scale flooding during the months of heaviest rainfall.

All the planet's waters were well populated. The better part of their life forms would serve a hungry traveler well if they could be caught; a meeting with some of the others was less desirable.

Slow, murky pools and moving water alike hosted aquatic reptiles of great size and greater appetite as well as several species of highly venomous swimming snakes given to hitching rides on floating debris to sun themselves or hunt any small passengers the mass might contain, and there was little difference between a wet log and a raft or small boat to their strange senses.

Spring leeches made drinking hazardous anywhere a stream was relatively quiet or from any lake or pond. Slender as a thick thread and almost transparent when unfed, the seven-inch-long creatures coiled beneath or beside some rock or other firmly anchored object and waited for an animal to bring its head near the water. When one did, the hunters sprang, seeking to enter the nostrils or mouth and fix themselves, or to attach themselves farther down in the throat, there to remain until they drank their fill of blood. At that point, the bloated creatures would drop off, pass unharmed through the digestive system, and begin their search for a new hunting ground, which was usually readily available in the wet world that had spawned them. Mating took place in the water, and development of the young did not require an intermediate host.

Faster, clearer stretches presented their own perils. These were chiefly navigational, but parts of many midsize and larger rivers were ruled by several species of closely related fish known collectively as sawmills. There were five kinds in all ranging from eight inches to two feet in length, all similar in general appearance and almost identical in behavior. They were either dark gray or dull brown in color with short, chunky bodies and heavy, strong heads dominated by powerful, protruding jaws.

The latter were armed with razor-keen, triangular teeth, three rows of them, that could sever a mouthful of flesh almost in the moment they closed on a target. The fish congregated in large schools, and when hungry or when blood tainted the water in sufficient volume, the whole shoal was thrown into a feeding frenzy that could strip a sixty-pound capa to the bones in less than a minute's time.

Varn can feel most things! Warn us! The gurry was sitting up on Islaen's knee, her bright eyes fixed on him. *Bandit will help! Bandit can scout for friends!*

The man smiled. *You always help, small one, and to good purpose, but there should be no need for you to do a great deal on this one. We will be traveling in very efficient company and can leave the worries to them, until we near target, at least.*

Why's Varn afraid?

I am not really.

But, Varn . . .

I do not like the thought of venturing into such country, he responded quickly, then continued more thoughtfully. *I do not trust it or myself within it, but I am not in terror of Amazoon of Indra. Only a fool would not accord a potential adversary of such power the respect it merits. If I am reacting more strongly than our comrades, it is only that I have less experience in wild country to support me.*

He caught himself. *I am sorry, Bandit. I was speaking more to myself than to you.*

Bandit understands! Varn's worried he won't be able to protect us all if things go wrong!

Something like that. —Be quiet now, small one. I do not want to disturb Islaen with this.

Yes, Varn!

True to her word, the little hen snuggled down in the Colonel's lap. Islaen's hands automatically cupped over her as she continued her conversation with Simon.

Sogan relaxed. If Islaen had been aware of their exchange at all, she had been engrossed enough in what Salombo was saying that she had not realized the nature of it. For that, he was grateful. She had enough to concern her in the mission ahead of them without having to shoulder his nerves as well, as she would inevitably do if he were careless enough to allow her to become aware of his feelings.

Scowling, he turned his attention to their comrades across the aisle. Bethe was dozing, in company with most of the transport's other passengers. Jake was watching the canopy flowing by below them, even as he was.

Varn's eyes narrowed, hardened. There was no sign of unease or displeasure on the redheaded Commando, just a lively interest that was only whetted by a respectful appreciation of the unique challenges and perils of this lush world to which they had been sent.

Why should it be otherwise, the former Admiral thought sourly. Karmikel was a veteran of this kind of work. He had encountered savage, hostile terrain often enough in the past and always proved the equal of it. That was reason enough to be confident of his ability to do so now.

Varn Tarl Sogan came close to hating him for that, although the Noreenan had proven himself to be a sound friend. Before that fateful encounter on Visnu of Brahmin, his own life had centered in space, on the great battleships of the Arcturian Navy and later on the *Fairest Maid*, the little needle-nose he had made his own after having been cast into the Federation after the War's close. He excelled there, but he knew he was still no match for either Islaen Connor or the man who had been her comrade since they had first entered Basic training, the man who had once loved her and had sought marriage with her . . .

Sogan shook his head angrily. This whining was unworthy, of himself and of Karmikel. Jake was no vacuum-brained shooting star. No Commando was. That kind did not survive. He was not eager to get into those treelands, either, even if he was less leery of them and of his own potential performance.

He sighed then. This was purposeless. Like the prospect or not, there was no avoiding the trek ahead of them. He might as well accept that with reasonably good grace as befitted one of his race and caste. It would be unpleasant but not deadly, not unless he and his comrades blew their part at the confrontation at its end.

It would be some time yet before the fast-flying transport reached their disembarkation point. His eyes closed. Rest time would be in short supply later. He would do well to use what was given to him now rather than squander it like this in worthless brooding.

THREE

THE WAR PRINCE became aware of Islaen's excitement and finished rousing out of the light sleep on whose borders he still hovered.

She felt him wake, and her mind touched his to share her delight. *I'm glad you're up, Varn. I didn't want you to miss this.*

His breath caught as he glanced out the window in response to her prompting. A range of mountains was rising up in the distance far ahead. They were tall enough that ice glinted like blue-white fire on their uppermost peaks, no mean feat on a planet as close to her sun-star as Amazoon of Indra, and they appeared to be young, for even the heavy, ever-changing growth covering all their slopes could not conceal their sharp, steep profile.

They also formed a nigh-unto solid wall. As nearly as he could estimate from this vantage, the nearest approach to a pass had to be at least nine to ten thousand feet high. The on-worlders had been entirely accurate in naming this the Barrier Ridge.

Magnificent, he whispered. The mountains held him utterly. The whole scene had that aura of unreality that distance often bequeaths to a sight that is both exquisitely lovely and awesome, and that magic, in consort with the mountains' beauty and power, lay its spell on him. For the first time since planeting on Amazoon, he felt drawn to the green world, able and willing to feel with and for her.

Varn broadened his mind link to include Bandit. None of the

three spoke but rather shared the quiet pleasure of this moment and the unanticipated beauty before them.

The Barrier Ridge did not appear any less fair as the transport drew closer to it, but the formidable nature of the mighty stone wall became even more evident as the detail made invisible by distance came into focus.

The former Admiral's thoughts slowly withdrew behind his shields once more. The bridge of a starship might be his true element, but he could handle any machine, particularly any machine that flew, expertly enough that his comrades almost invariably yielded the place at the controls to him. He understood surplanetary conditions that could affect such craft, and there was much that he saw here that he did not like at all.

His eyes narrowed as their vessel began climbing on its approach to the pass that was their gate to the vast southern jungles. The potential for disaster existed here, and if their hosts were as good as they were purported to be, they would be even more acutely aware of that fact than he was.

He turned to Salombo. "Do you take transports over that wall very often, Sergeant?" he asked quietly.

The Amazoonan stopped himself from voicing the retort that sprang to his lips. He knew enough of men to realize that one did not make that sort of answer to the Commando-Captain. Besides, the question was a legitimate one and merited a direct answer. "Not these," he admitted. "We usually use high-altitude, two-man scouts, but we figured a single, low-flying craft'd have a better chance of slipping in past the intruder's guards."

"It could be more maneuverable for these heights," he observed.

Simon shrugged, but he regarded the off-worlder with greater respect. "We won't be up here long enough to get into trouble," he assured him. "The Ridge is notorious for freak drafts and currents, right enough, but Milo's a good pilot. He'll get us through and back again, the Green Lady willing."

And fortune, Sogan thought. He merely nodded, however. It might not take a very practiced eye to see that the transport did not have the maneuverability of a Commando flier or the ability to climb quickly or very high to break out of a bad crosscurrent, but neither was it a limping cripple. These

Amazoonans wanted to complete this job and get home again quickly with as little excitement as possible, and they sure as space should know what they were doing flying the sky of their own planet . . .

Islaen Connor stirred in her seat. *They're not worried, Varn. I'd have picked that up long since if they were.*

This was not the insubstantial discomfort he had felt earlier, and he was not embarrassed that she had detected it. *I just figured I would ask all the same,* he told her dryly.

The woman smiled. *I don't think you're ever completely happy when anyone but yourself has the controls, Admiral.*

Arcturian officers are accustomed to carrying their commands physically as well as verbally, Colonel Connor.

Bandit whistled and nudged Islaen's hand to get her attention. *Varn's not scared, Islaen!* she informed her. *He's just being careful!*

That confirms it, Sogan told her. *Our winged comrade is perceptive.*

Yes!

The Noreenan laughed. *Perceptive when she supports you. Something rather less flattering when she reveals thoughts you'd prefer to keep screened.*

Bandit's been good! the gurry protested.

Aye, love, so you have.

Recently, at least, the war prince amended, recalling the several occasions when her revelations had set his face burning.

Varn! Islaen warned. *Don't tease her. You know how she tries to please you.*

I do, indeed. He ran his finger under the gurry's chin and was rewarded by a rumbling purr. *She succeeds remarkably well.*

They fell into a comfortable silence after that and concentrated on what was going on around them. The transport had finished climbing and was passing through the gap that had been their target. It was flying very low, only about three hundred feet above the canopy, as much as this stage to lessen the effect of the fierce wind buffeting it as to reduce the chance of detection by their enemies. That last should be no threat for two or three hours yet.

The Commando-Colonel watched the scene below in fascination. So much detail was visible from here. She could all but see the wild things scampering and flitting among the leaves, and she longed for Varn's talent to receive their transmissions, their feelings, at least those of the higher-level creatures. It seemed a far more pleasurable gift than her own. The readings she took from humans and their equals were all too often dark and violent, filled with hate and the lust for blood . . .

The Arcturian stiffened beside her. "Light your burners, damn you, and lift!"

In the moment it took to glance from his tense face back to the window, the dive he had already noticed had become all too perceptible. The transport was no longer skimming over the trees. It was hurtling directly into them.

FOUR

I'LL DIE HERE, the woman thought even as she dove for the floor, instinctively clutching Bandit to her so that her body might serve as a shield for the little Jadite.

There was a vast shuddering, then a bounce followed by two others. They seemed oddly soft, far away, the noise accompanying them muted.

Intense heat and fire followed fast, filling all the air above her. Her hair was singeing—she could smell it. She could smell burning flesh as well, strongly enough that she gagged on the reek, but that was not hers. The exposed skin of her neck was blistering, but other than that, she was as yet untouched.

She had to get out, get the others out! Islaen frantically looked for her consort and found him. Simon had fallen or had been thrown across Sogan. The Amazoonan was stunned. His right cheek was ripped open and bleeding profusely, his forehead and face were badly scorched. Varn was struggling to free himself of the Sergeant's weight but appeared to be all right; the bigger man's body had shielded him from the blast.

Daylight showed ahead, not far ahead. *Get him clear!* she commanded. *I've got our packs.*

Without a word, he hastened to obey, keeping low to avoid as much as possible the flames licking all around them.

Bandit freed herself from the woman's hold. *Islaen! Jake's hurt! Bethe, too! Help them!*

I will! Fly now yourself!

The Colonel turned swiftly toward their comrades' seats. Karmikel was unconscious from a blow that had gashed his scalp so deeply that the bone of his skull was exposed. Bethe

24

Danlo was trying desperately to bring him out, working almost exclusively with her right arm. The left appeared to be broken.

She leaped to the demolitions expert's aid. Together, they manhandled Jake out of the seat and dragged him along the aisle.

The distance they had to go was short, only two rows beyond their own, and the fire, though present everywhere and increasing in violence with each passing moment, did not have the intensity of the initial blast, which had originated in the fuel-rich nose. If they kept moving fast and watched what was happening around them, they should escape with only minor scorching.

Sogan met them at the opening, the place where the tail section had broken from the rest of the transport. He lowered Karmikel the five feet to the ground and then the injured Bethe.

Islaen tossed down the packs her training had made her keep with her. "The renewer's in mine," she told the blond woman. "Use it on yourself and the others."

With that, she darted back inside the ruined vehicle. The talent that allowed her to receive and decipher the emotions of fellow humans had told her that some traces of life remained within. It was only a flickering in each case and would not continue long—another aspect of her gift detected the nature and severity of injuries and even of some illnesses—but she could not leave still-living beings to the flames, however hopeless the final outcome might be for them.

She bit her lip. The heat seemed, was, worse, and so was the smell. She did not believe the fire was hot enough to be feeding on the bodies directly, but their clothes were burning and the seat padding, and a lot of charring of flesh was taking place in consequence.

The war prince reached her before she had half begun the crawl back. *Which ones?* he asked grimly.

Two in the seats in front of ours.

Still alive? There was no point to this if they were not.

Aye.

Three rows had come off with the tail, and it took but a few moments to reach the survivors, a man and a woman, both so badly burned that it seemed impossible that either could still be living. Of a certainty, they would be able to give no help to their rescuers.

Fortunately, the transport's seats had been scaled to accommodate Amazoon's race and were wide with good room for long legs between the rows, and they were able to lift the pair out quickly, first jerking aside the body in the outer seat. Quickly but with little gentleness. Had both not been deeply comatose, they might well not have survived that phase of the rescue, agonizingly injured as they were.

Sogan shuddered as a layer of skin peeled away in his hands. It would have been better for them had they died in the initial blast like the rest of their comrades. He did not require Islaen Connor's gift to recognize that neither was going to live long, not without immediate treatment of a kind his party was powerless to give them. Even if rescuers were already en route to them, he doubted they could be gotten to a hospital and under regrowth treatment in time.

Whatever about that, he could no more leave them to perish here than could the Commando-Colonel. He took a firm hold on the larger of the two victims, the male, and started dragging him forward.

A tongue of flame spurted out suddenly and licked across his jaw before he could jerk his head away. He swore savagely but then made himself ignore the pain. It was a minor hurt easily remedied. To remain here longer nursing it was to invite the fate of the near corpse whose end he was striving to ease.

The Noreenan had to wait until her comrade had moved his charge out of her way. She used those seconds to dive for Jake's and Bethe's packs and slung both on top of the woman in her care. All their lives could depend on their contents . . .

Tears of pain smarted in her eyes. Would Varn never move?

The fire was not actually touching her, but the heat of it was acting on the burns she had already taken in this rescue attempt, intensifying them, and the air was getting ever harder to breathe, fouler and hotter. If she hit an exceptionally virulent pocket—or pulled in a lungful of actual flame—she was done. She would either collapse from the poison or see her nose, throat, and lungs seared. That last, the renewer could not repair.

Sogan was well down the aisle. Islaen tugged at the Amazoonan's inert body. It was hard to get it moving. The injured woman was both a great deal heavier and taller than herself.

She would not let go and give it up, and she dared not allow herself to delay any further, so she steeled herself and grimly kept going. This was not the hardest thing she had ever done, and she would not have to continue with it for long . . .

Someone shouldered past her. Jake!

"This is a job for someone with real muscle, Colonel."

"Someone who had to be carried out himself!" she retorted, but she let him at it, satisfying herself with lifting the victim's legs to ease and guide the withdrawal.

Seconds later she was on the ground with her consort's arm around her as he hurried her away from the blazing transport.

Islaen Connor turned again once she had put some distance between herself and the wreck. She realized with something of a shock that it had only been a matter of minutes since the crash.

Now for the first time she had the chance to take stock of their situation.

The transport had broken into two pieces. The front, the larger section, was an inferno. The craft's fuel supply had spurred the flames into a fury that nothing could approach or survive. It was badly crumpled as well, and the impact had probably given mercifully quick deaths at least to the pilot and those in the forward couple of rows. No one was alive in there at this point.

The rear section was not blazing nearly as fiercely, and it had remained more nearly intact. Fate had spared the off-worlders by placing them there and in the very rearmost seats.

Maybe spared them only temporarily. The guerrilla glanced nervously at the greenery all around them. Where could they flee, exhausted as they were and with gravely injured comrades, if all this went up? They would never be able to move fast enough.

She relaxed on that score in the next moment. Whatever their other worries, this need not be added to them. The vegetation right beneath and beside the transport had taken fire, of course, but the whole area was simply too wet for the rest to follow suit. If the flames should begin to dry out the neighboring shrubbery sufficiently to imperil it the daily rains even now threatening to burst from darkening clouds would cool them off enough to withstand the challenge until the conflagration at last burned itself out.

"Here, Islaen. You can use a dose of this."

The Noreenan gave Bethe a tight smile and took from her what appeared at first glance to be a heavy, antique hand blaster. Within seconds, the burns and blisters vanished from her body as if they had never been.

The renewer ray was one of medicine's greatest discoveries, providing almost instantaneous, complete regeneration of damaged or destroyed skin, muscles, blood vessels, even nerves and bone. Only the organs of the chest and abdominal cavities could not be so repaired, requiring treatment with the much newer and far more complex regrowth equipment.

At the War's beginning, only a few of the great experimental hospitals could support the then-massive renewer systems, but development had progressed quickly until they became standard equipment on every major battleship, and then on the medium-class and many of the smaller-class vessels as well. Now Federation scientists had produced a model portable enough to be used by individuals or small mobile parties such as her unit, which was one of the first teams chosen to benefit from and test it in the field. It had saved their lives and permitted them to continue as an effective unit on more than one mission already and would help them again in the wake of this accident. At least, her team would be strong and sound to face whatever still lay ahead of them.

Your turn, she told the former Admiral, who had remained beside her since leading her away from the wreck. He might have kept quiet about it verbally and in mind while he was helping her treat her more difficult to reach injuries, but he was hurting, too.

Thanks, Colonel. He turned somberly to the place where their comrades were settling the other two survivors. *It will not be of much help to them, I am afraid.*

She shook her head. *No, except to give them relief from the burns. Internal injuries will finish both of them, before morning, I expect.* They needed a regrowth, and with the transport's normal and emergency transceivers burned, they had no hope of calling in rescuers to carry them to one in time.

Bandit had been hovering unhappily by the dying Rangers but now flew to her comrades. *Islaen will help?*

I can't, love, not this time. They need a lot more than we can do for them. —You're all right yourself?

Bandit's fine! No burns! See!

She swooped in a graceful, arching circle around the woman before settling on her shoulder. *Bandit's glad we're safe!*

Aye, love. Fortune flew with us today.

Islaen frowned suddenly. "Where's Simon?" she called aloud.

Even as she spoke, she cast her mind out. Searing agony met her. "The transport! He's gone back into the tail!"

All four guerrillas raced for the wreck, but before they could reach it, the Sergeant staggered out again and tumbled to the ground, dragging two large, charred bundles after him.

He was terribly burned, but he was conscious and raised a mutilated hand to stop Jake from turning the renewer on him. "Don't waste the charge, Commando."

"It's self-regenerating, requiring a recharge only every twelve months, or before each mission if you're a worrier like Islaen. —Have you a black hole for a brain to go back in there . . ."

"Let him be, Jake," Islaen Connor told him softly. "He wouldn't have done it if he didn't think it was necessary."

The healing ray was already doing its work, and Salombo nodded more vigorously, although he still made no attempt to raise himself to a sitting position. "Survival kits. We'll need them to get back and even more if you decide to go ahead. The distance's about the same either way."

He rested while he watched his fingers regenerate from charred stumps. "A marvelous plaything, that," he commented, then fixed his eyes back on the two bundles. "Each of those holds an inflatable boat, a tarpaulin, hammock nets, an axe and saw, a couple of knives, food and medical supplies, directional gear plus some good maps, and a small solar-powered transceiver."

The Ranger grimaced. "They 're strong enough to pierce the canopy, assuming they've survived intact, but I wouldn't advise using them. They're meant to reach just about everything on the planet. The intruders'll probably get a call before our own people would. That won't help our comrades, and you can put credits down that they'll guess our purpose for being here real fast after that business with the scout. They'll lift for sure then, and you'll never get them."

His eyes closed. "The coverings are fire shielded. The surface coating's cooked, but the insides should be safe."

He seemed to steel himself and sat up. "Much better! —I left my own map over there, by your gear, just in case I didn't make it back out. Let's collect it and then see about setting up camp. It's late now, and we will have to rest before tackling anything else."

FIVE

THE COLONEL'S EYES shadowed when they came to the place where the other Amazoonans were lying. She knelt beside the woman she had struggled to save and made a show of feeling the side of her neck for the pulse she already knew was not there. The man was still holding his own. She pointed to the corpse and shook her head.

Without a word, Karmiḳel lifted the body and laid it beneath a tree near the transport.

He returned to find the others had already unwrapped the surplanetary survival gear and were hastily using the tarps to fashion a shelter for themselves. At nearly nine thousand feet, the air was chilly anyway, and the threatening rain had at last begun to fall with a sullen determination that quickly soaked them and set them shivering violently, though shock, too, was playing a part in that.

A fire and some food put them to rights again, and all five huddled together in silence in the cramped lean-to they had constructed, trying to put themselves back together after the trauma of the crash.

Islaen stroked Bandit comfortingly, but her eyes remained fixed on the fire in front of her. Right now, she wondered if any of their efforts would prove of worth . . .

Sogan's hand brushed her arm, and his mind gently touched hers. *You did all you could for her, my Islaen. You knew the course chartered for her when you pulled her out. We both did.*

Aye. —She was lucky in a way, I suppose. Her face tightened. *At least, we don't have to actively doom the other*

31

poor bloke. They had been spared that decision. Neither of the two transceivers was operational.

She sat up and flexed her shoulders to work the stiffness out of them. Other decisions did have to be made. The semiclandestine nature of their mission precluded the possibility of a very early hunt for them, nor would they be readily spotted in this place once a search did begin. The trees were short and sparse at this altitude in comparison with the lushness of their growth farther downslope and at sea level, but the transport had come down right among them, and the cover was more than thick enough to conceal almost all sign of the crash. If they were going to get help, they would have to do what the Ranger Yeoman had done before them—walk out. At the very least, they would have to get to some clearing where they might have a reasonable chance of signaling craft passing overhead.

They did have no other choice. As Simon Salombo had mentioned, they could try to do what they had been sent to Amazoon of Indra to accomplish. They had made it about halfway to target, and the Commando unit had survived intact. The actual assault had been their assignment from the beginning. The Jungle Rangers had only been sent out to guide and support them.

Fulfilling their mission would be difficult, but it should not necessarily be their ultimate doom. With real luck, they might take a transceiver from the intruders, and if they failed in that, they still had their considerable wilderness skills and the equipment and supplies they had been fortunate enough to salvage. People had made it out of as bad or worse with a lot less before now. If they could not, well, Commandos had died in the line of duty since their inception. They accepted that risk when they entered the service.

The change in their commander's attitude communicated itself to the others.

Jake seemed to read the direction of her thoughts. "We're to go ahead with it?" he asked calmly.

"If Simon thinks it's possible. And sensible. We mightn't actually be saving anything in terms of time by going on."

The Amazoonan had been dozing but had roused himself at the sound of Karmikel's voice. Now, he nodded at the question implicit in the Colonel's answer. "It's reasonable. We're just about over the Ridge, and the way down's easy. It's a brisk, physically tough climb," he amended, "but not technically very difficult save in one place. You'd need mountaineering skill on a large scale to go back north, and you'd move real slow without the equipment to match it. Our Yeoman managed it, but she had no other choice."

"You believe we can make it through to target?" Varn Tarl Sogan pressed. "In condition to fight?"

"Yes, given reasonable luck, of course, and assuming we don't make too many stupid mistakes. The jungle doesn't forgive error readily and has no patience whatsoever with fools."

He unfolded the map he had brought with him of the approach to their destination and lay it beside the more general ones he had rescued along with the other survival gear.

"We were to have set down in this big clearing and then move out cross-country. It'll be necessary to take to the water now, pick up the Maiden down at the foot of this gap where we are and follow it until it joins with the Matron. That'll carry us as near as we can ride to target, closer, in fact, than we would've come by air. We'll be glad of that saving when we reach this bend and have to leg it."

"How long will all this take?" the Commando-Colonel asked wearily. Even on the maps, it looked like a phenomenal amount of very rough country that they had to cover.

Simon only shrugged. "That depends on the river's condition. Both have their share of pitfalls for smaller craft like ours, and we've had a lot of rain to feed them for this time of year. You can count on several days' hard traveling anyway."

The former Admiral was studying the charts closely. "Apart from our descent here, the bulk of this appears to be fairly level country."

"Sure. Sea level."

"It is normal jungle by Amazoon's standards? No tangles or heavy undergrowth?"

"Very little except by the rivers and in the odd clearing." He eyed the off-worlder. "What are you thinking, Captain Sogan?"

"The river journey will not be a fast or an easy one. Those waterways are so convoluted that we shall have to cover three, four times the actual distance. The most direct course would be overland from here if it could be done."

The other shook his head. "That center portion's prime leech country, Captain. If you never believe another word I say, trust that you do not want to venture there."

Varn thought to himself that he did not want to venture anywhere on this accursed planet, but he met Salombo's eyes steadily. "Could it be endured for the sake of the days we would gain? Every hour we lose increases the risk that our quarry will lift before we reach them."

"Could Visnu's ravagers be endured?" Jake Karmikel asked sourly.

Islaen fixed him with a wilting glare before giving her attention back to the other men. "It's a good question. What about it, Sergeant?"

"Not if you want to arrive fit to do much fighting," he told them with a certainty that closed the subject for all of them.

The gurry, who had been reading the feelings backing Simon's statement, gave a shrill whistle. *Horrible place! Let's leave! Go home to Thorne!*

Quiet, Bandit! Sogan commanded sharply. *We have work to do. This council is to decide the best way to go about that. There can be no question of quitting without making the attempt.*

Yes, Varn, she replied meekly. *But Bandit still doesn't like it!*

Neither do I. —And do not repeat that.

Bandit won't, Varn!

His eyes flickered back to the others. Most of their discussion had been conducted in whispers so as not to distract Islaen, but if she had heard more than Bandit's initial protest, she gave no sign of it. All three of them had become adept at concealing their mental conversations from those around them.

"If all that area is infested, what hope at all do we have on the climb down and in the thickets? Nowhere will we be in closer contact with the vegetation where they live."

"The leeches we have to worry about don't like high country, and they stay out of the tangles and low growth almost completely. Too many crown wasps too close."

"Crown wasps?" Islaen Connor asked. Their notes had been vague about those, had scarcely mentioned them, in fact.

"Your reports wouldn't cover them. They don't affect ground parties.

"The name actually covers a number of species, how many

we're not yet certain. Each is specific to a certain type or very closely related types of tree, but they're all small, and their habits are similar. They think nothing's better than leeches for brooding and maintaining their young and actively hunt the blood suckers out. That's what keeps their populations under reasonable control.

"They live among the leaves of their chosen plants, which have adapted to meet their needs by providing hollow branches or loosely connected bark so that the smaller insects can find ready nesting sites. Those supporting larger varieties have rough bark to anchor the nests they fashion out of a substance, a sort of waterproof paper, that they secrete. In return, the crown wasps give excellent protection from leaf cutters and other such marauders. When their trees happen to be seedlings and saplings, then the wasps are close to the ground as well, and their prey naturally make themselves somewhat scarce.

"Warm-blooded creatures're normally of no interest to them, but if they get the idea that their nests're threatened, they'll attack anything. They're little fellows, and in moderation, their stings won't greatly inconvenience one not actually sensitive to their venom after the initial discomfort passes off, but a swarm attack is another matter entirely."

"We'll be careful not to provoke one," the Colonel promised. She did not mind wasps. Her own Noreen sported many kinds of them, and they rarely bothered anyone unless they were purposely or accidentally aroused. She did not even mind leeches, not theoretically at any rate. They were but beasts filling a peculiar place in nature's scheme. She wanted no meetings with either of them nonetheless and was resolved to make very well sure that none occurred.

The discussion went on for well over an hour longer. Simon seemed determined to press all the information he could, all the jungle and river lore he possessed, on the Commandos, and for their part, the off-worlders wanted to try to lay a few tentative plans and counterplans for the assault on the renegade camp. Whether the mysterious intruders were those they had come seeking or not, they had shown themselves to be both well armed and all too willing to use those weapons. It behooved the Federation party to be as well prepared as possible when the time came to challenge them.

At last, Islaen put an end to the talk. They were all

emotionally and physically exhausted and in need of rest more than even knowledge.

Tired as she was, the Commando-Sergeant crept away from the others to stand awhile beside Jake Karmikel, who had drawn the first watch. She shivered in the damp air and folded her arms about herself for warmth, although no such gesture, no fire, could drive out the chill that gripped her when she thought of the escape they had had. It had been so close . . .

Jake saw how her fingers unconsciously massaged her left arm. "Does it still hurt?" he asked in concern. "Another few seconds under the renewer . . ."

"No need," she replied, smiling quickly up at him. "I'm sound out." She grew grave. "Think where we'd be without that portable ray, Jake. I'd be stuck with a broken arm for the duration, and you'd be in worse shape still. Even Varn and Islaen wouldn't be feeling so spry. They both took some hefty surface burns."

"We wouldn't be planning a journey downriver, sure as space is black." He scowled. "Maybe that part of it wouldn't have been entirely to our disadvantage, either. The more I think about all this, the less appealing it seems."

"I'm glad to hear you say it, my friend. I thought I was the only one to feel like that."

"Space, no, woman! You can put credits down that our Admiral isn't at all happy about any of this, and I know damn well that Islaen isn't, however much she believes it's neces- sary. As for Bandit, I'm nearly certain Sogan quashed a full-fledged protest from her back there."

The spacer chuckled sympathetically. "Poor little pet! She's the only one of us with the sense to speak her mind at a time like this."

"Aye, and she's always right, too," he agreed glumly. "When she calls something a bad idea, it inevitably is, at least from the standpoint of our health and well-being."

Karmikel slipped his arm around her. He, too, was aware of the narrowness of their escape. The Grim Commandant had put his hand on both of them. That he had loosed his hold again, left them to each other, was a reprieve scarcely to be believed. He kissed her tenderly, vowing within his soul not to waste any of the time so nearly miraculously restored to them.

Bethe shivered again under the lash of the night air. He released her. "Better go inside and knock out while you can, lass. Your turn out here will come all too soon."

Islaen Connor woke slowly. She could not say what had penetrated the chains of sleep clasping her save that she felt uneasy, as if something was badly wrong.

Moving carefully so as not to disturb Bandit, who was curled against her beneath the spider silk blanket from her pack, she finally sat up and tried to take stock of their camp.

Varn was lying beside her, his face just visible in the dim glow of the fire. He looked drawn and tired but appeared to be sleeping peacefully. His surface transmissions confirmed that this was indeed so, but all the inner part of his mind was closed.

That was hardly surprising. Between the camp and chill and the stress of the day, his back had to be bothering him. Even a full month of renewer treatment had not been able to completely erase the scars left by the Arcturian executioners, and they still occasionally gave him minor trouble. He was too much a warrior to complain of that, nor could she fault him. She would not broadcast it, either, if it were her problem.

She gave a half-loving, half-exasperated shake of her head. She knew her man full well. He was concealing more than mild physical discomfort. Varn Tarl Sogan did not enjoy being bested, much less the prospect of actually proving inferior, incapable, in a given situation. He could endure if he did not like the fact that she and Jake Karmikel were his masters in a wilderness but not that he might not be able to carry his part, that he might fail her and their other comrades.

She had no fear of that. The war prince was now far better in the wild than he himself believed, more than capable of functioning as a full and important member of the unit. She gave her head another shake. That strange combination of pride and genuine humility was as much a part of him as his courage and gentleness. It was up to her to work with and around it.

The Commando-Colonel's mind slipped away from him. Karmikel was next to Sogan, wrapped in the sleep of the just. Her eyes sparkled at the sight of him. That man proved out the claim that a Commando could sleep anywhere. She had often teased him that he could drop off while up to his neck in a pool of icy rainwater. At any rate, there certainly was nothing amiss with him.

Bethe Danlo was outside on watch. She was cold and none too happy about her present situation save for her gratitude that the rain had stopped. Otherwise, all was right with her as well.

Islaen's mind swept the surrounding area to confirm that there were no human-level intruders trying to slip up on the camp, then returned to her immediate surroundings.

She had been postponing this part of her examination but now forced her thoughts to reach out to the Ranger Varn had pulled from the burning transport. As she expected, she met only a void. It was a shell that lay there now. The man who had animated it was gone.

Her head bowed in a quick prayer, then raised again. Her look was bleak, filled with a bitter regret for the help she had been unable to render.

Soon, her thoughts returned to her own situation. She was still vaguely troubled. It was never pleasant to lose a companion, but this outcome had been inevitable from the start. Why should she be more acutely conscious of his passing than she had been of that woman's earlier? Why should the feeling continue now that she had identified its source?

Her heart went cold. It was not the poor Jungle Ranger's death or any human or animal activity around the camp that was bothering her. It was, rather, an absence, a lacking.

Simon? "Simon!"

The two male guerrillas woke with a start even as the demolitions expert dashed back to the shelter.

"What in all the hells is the matter . . ." Jake began angrily, but he stopped himself when he saw her kneeling over the big man. "Islaen?"

"Dead," she whispered hoarsely. "He's just died."

"Dead! How . . ."

"His lungs were seared. The renewer bought him a bit more time, but he was doomed as surely as the other two we lost."

Tears welled in Bethe's eyes. "He knew it. That's why he went back into the fire for that gear."

"And then used the time he had left to pass on all the information he could to us," Varn agreed. "A brave man."

"Too brave!" Jake snapped. "With the help of the renewer, we might have been able to keep him going just long enough if we'd started back at once. —Islaen, where in space were your blasted gifts all this time? How could you have let that man die?"

"Put it on freeze, Karmikel!" the war prince snarled. "You know damn well that she could not examine him while he was conscious. It is not an imperceptible process like thought reception. She might have done it anyway had she suspected something was wrong, but he took great care that we should not realize he was injured just so we would not be tempted to scrub the attack."

The redhead's eyes fell. "Sorry, lass. I was off the charts. Not even Bandit knew he'd been hurt."

Nooo! the gurry averred miserably.

"It's not your fault either, little girl," he told her, reading her unhappiness readily from the tone of her accompanying whistle. "I just find the thought of letting a dying man put up our lean-to hard to stomach, that's all."

His hands balled. "Let's make good and sure that we blast that space scum to stardust when we find them. They're the ultimate cause of all this, and I want them to die for it, every last son of a Scythian ape of them."

SIX

WHEN ENOUGH OF the dawn light pierced the canopy to allow them to function, the Federation soldiers lay the three dead Rangers inside the shell of the transport with their fellows to await the arrival of a cremation detail in accordance with Amazoonan death custom. That done, they set about dismantling their camp and preparing themselves for the long trek ahead.

Varn hoisted his pack to his shoulders with a grunt. It was a load. Islaen had, as usual, insisted that they travel fully supplied despite the intended short duration of the assignment, and they were bringing away all of the salvaged Amazoonan gear as well.

He grimaced as he settled the burden more comfortably. There was no arguing with the wisdom of that. They might need only a single boat and her equipment, but they dared not abandon the other, given the possibility that one of them might have suffered damage in the crash or the even greater chance of running into misfortune on the river. The things were plaguey heavy, however, and he was not looking forward to lugging the vessel in his charge on what would have been a strenuous downslope scramble for an unburdened man.

The two transceivers were coming as well, each in the care of one of the women. Neither had been totally wrecked, and there was a strong possibility that if they were cannibalized and worked upon with a lot of creative improvision, a functioning unit might be produced. They would be very glad of the chance to summon an airlift home by the time they had accomplished their purpose, assuming they proved equal to that task at all.

His eyes darkened until they seemed almost black. If they did not accomplish it, in all likelihood, they would be requiring no service at all save that which their poor companions in the transport were awaiting.

"Collecting stardust, Admiral?"

He looked down at Bethe Danlo. "Just thinking, Sergeant."

Her pack seemed as large as herself, although she appeared to be carrying it with no greater trouble than he was having with his own. "Are you sure you are going to be able to manage that thing? The descent will be fairly rugged according to Salombo."

"Admiral Sogan, I was carting cargo around my father's freighter when I was ten years old," she told him tartly but with complete good humor. The pack was double its normal bulk, and she knew what she must look like with it on. "I guess I'm a rather odd sight," she admitted ruefully.

He smiled but decided it was wiser not to follow up on that one. "I was more concerned that it might prove too unwieldy, that all of them might for that matter."

"We'll have to do it in two trips, then, so pray they don't. —Uh-oh, our commander's giving us the move-out sign."

Islaen Connor had raised her own burden and waved to her companions to begin. Karmikel fell in immediately in her wake.

Sogan and the demolitions expert followed after them. It was a conscious positioning on the part of both, although neither would have admitted that. They were hoping that they might benefit from the greater experience of the leaders, watch their movements and learn about and avoid any particular difficulties they encountered.

They remained silent for the first four hundred yards, then Bethe sighed. "It's rough already," she remarked glumly.

"That will not change."

She glanced up at the Arcturian. "Those two have spent almost their whole adult lives at this sort of thing, but we're essentially spacers. —Do you think we'll be able to pull it, Varn?"

"We must, Bethe Danlo," he replied grimly. "We are completely without any other option."

The descent proved nastier than Islaen had anticipated. As they had been warned, the slope was steep, much of it extremely so, although it rarely degenerated into an actual cliff. The sheerest spots, they bypassed at the cost of much extra walking and scrambling; their worst problem was to see them in the first place. Locating drops and other pitfalls in time to avoid them was not always easy, particularly at the highest altitudes. There, the trees were thinner and farther spaced than in the flatter country below, and the added measure of Indra's light gave rise to a comparatively rich ground cover. Only the fact that the harsher climate on the slopes limited the number and density of floor-level species prevented the area from becoming one vast tangle.

That difficulty lessened with every foot they came down, but another inexorably took its place. One could work well and hard in the brisk temperatures of the heights. In the unrelenting heat and humidity of Amazoon's lowlands, every movement, every soggy breath, was an effort.

The Noreenan woman's clothes were soaked with sweat. They were uncomfortable against her skin and would grow even more so as the hours dragged by. It was not pleasant to realize that she had but the one spare set and after she changed into that, there would be no more dry clothing until they were finished with this accursed mission and back in Amazoon's capital. Only Bandit, with her natural covering and her ability to use it to adjust her body temperature, would escape this particular misery, at least the worst of it. Even she was not going to be able to deflect all the effects of the jungle planet's execrable climate.

Perpetually wet garments was a hardship, not a danger, unless they were careless enough to permit fungus infections to develop on their moist, covered skin. There were other things of more immediate concern.

Her mind touched her husband's. *Any wildlife in evidence, Varn?*

Plenty, he responded, joining his receptors with hers so that she could experience for herself what he was describing. *Nothing very large, but there are a lot of creatures around us.*

As was the case on every world giving rise to life forms, most were very low on the intelligence scale, and all the war prince could detect of them was the bare fact that they existed. Even of the others, the best he could read from the majority were those basic, powerful drive emotions common to just about all living beings—hunger, fear, pain, strong anticipation and triumph, keen disappointment, relief, as if after an escape. Only a comparatively few of Amazoon's native denizens were advanced enough, with minds similar enough to a human's, that he could receive more specific information from them.

Those did abound, too, but most were in the tree crowns far above, and as nearly as he could tell, not many seemed to be of any significant size to judge by their mental complexity—though Bandit was proof that possession of high intelligence was no infallible test of size.

Large or small, those taking note of the Federation party invariably did so shyly, curiously perhaps, but showing no desire to approach the off-worlders.

Islaen nodded, satisfied, and withdrew again to return to her own work of guiding the company and scanning the area around them for the unanticipated but never-to-be-ignored possibility of human presence.

Varn carefully raised and set his shields. He did not wish to burden her with some of the thoughts troubling him.

None of Amazoon's higher animals bothered him. In truth, he liked most of the touches he was receiving from those unseen dwellers of the treetops. They were free, clean, primal, reassuring because they were what should be coming from the offspring of this vibrant planet that had given them birth.

It was the vastly more numerous marginal contacts that made him uneasy. More than uneasy. He cringed at some of those touches.

The predator's claw, the serpent's fang, the wasp's sting, the spider's bite, those he could accept as he had once accepted the pletzar banks on a Federation warship. With the parasites, it was different. The six- and eight-legged varieties were bad enough, but the leeches and the several external and internal near mimics of them, those revolted him. When he felt the eagerness of their response to the presence of his unit, he wanted to vomit.

It was not fear, not as he had known for Mirelle's nightmare fungus or for Visnu's ravager armies, which had well nigh been a walking death for the entire colony trying to establish itself there and even more nearly his own death. No threat of that magnitude existed on Amazoon of Indra. There was always danger, aye. That was inevitable in any wilderness. Under certain circumstances, the jungle's hunters could become deadly to one or more members of even a careful party, but in no sense did they represent the vast, all-encompassing threat blighting some other planets.

They would encounter no giants here such as haunted the equatorial treelands. He almost wished that they would. Those were a concrete menace, and he could have responded to them as enemies, avoided and, if necessary, fought them. That would have been clean, with the element of disgust overshadowed by real danger and the need to thwart it.

The war prince glanced down in response to an upsurge of frustration and flicked a four-inch, gray-thing off his sleeve.

He shuddered. Islaen looked upon these monstrosities as nothing more than another manifestation of natural adaptation, little though she might want them crawling all over her, but he could not bring himself to be so broad-minded. He had been bred in a palace and trained in space, and to him, such beasts were obscenities.

At least, he had little worry about finding any of them lodged on himself. The guerrillas had known from the beginning that they would be penetrating heavily infested territory and had prepared accordingly. Their precautions left them less comfortable than they might otherwise have been, but they were totally effective against their would-be tormentors.

Their pants fitted tightly into high boots that protected as well against the strike of a serpent, and their shirts were closed at the wrists. The jackets they kept on despite the heat were fastened all the way to the chin with the hoods raised to shield head and neck, a necessary safeguard since a leech's saliva anesthesized the wounds it made, allowing it to feed undetected. Only their faces and hands were open to assault, and those were easy enough to guard.

That last would hold true only until they approached the tangle abutting the river and they were forced to contend with the hordes of flying insects native to such places. Those would not be able to penetrate the sturdy, repellent-impregnated clothes, either, but there would be no holding them away from exposed flesh. They could not afford to squander their relatively small store of repellent unless and until the pressure on them became excessive to the point of danger or being outright unendurable.

At the moment, that thought did not trouble Sogan. Their shots had been augmented prior to the mission to prevent them from contracting any Amazoonan diseases, and any minor physical torment they might have to endure away from this place seemed preferable in his mind to this revolting persecution they were now undergoing, no matter how impotent it might actually be.

SEVEN

THE OFF-WORLDERS forced themselves on, each battling his discomfort and ever-growing dislike for Amazoon's most apparent wildlife as best he might.

The Arcturian felt exhausted. Already, only at the start of their march, every movement had become an effort that had to be forced from his body. His muscles ached, protesting the burden of the heavy pack. Even his chest, his lungs, hurt, and he had to will himself to go on drawing in and exhaling the soggy, unpleasantly scented air.

He fought to keep from staggering openly. His pride would not permit that, not while Jake Karmikel could keep going, if not quite with back unbowed, then at least steadily, with no sign of impending collapse.

Sogan allowed himself to drop into the fourth place in the line of march. If he should prove less than perfect at concealing his discomfort, his lapses would not be quite so noticeable here, but chiefly, he wanted to be in a position from which he could watch the progress of the others. Islaen and Bethe were both hefting burdens nearly the equal of his own, and their strength was less. They appeared to be bearing up, as well as he and Jake at any rate, but he wanted to hold himself ready to help if either ran into difficulty. At least, concentrating on that idea lifted him a little out of his own misery . . .

The worst of it all was the nagging knowledge that everything they were enduring might be for nothing. Salombo had stressed that one barrier lay between them and their goal that they might not be able to cross, heavily burdened and under-equipped as they were. The Yeoman had managed, but desperation had fired her, and she had been carrying no weight.

That would mean they must accept defeat and retrace their steps. There was weakness, cowardice, enough in him that the possibility was not entirely unappealing. From the sample he had already gotten of Amazoon's jungle, he would not be sorry to terminate his association with it as quickly as was feasible, especially since the return would be made without the heavy boat currently bending his shoulders.

Varn kept his thoughts to himself, although he guessed his comrades' would not be very different. None of the others were whining; he would not be the one to start.

The guerrillas ploughed on for another two miles, moving in all but total silence as much to conserve their strength as for security's sake.

They came to a halt, were forced to a halt. A seemingly solid wall of vegetation blocked the way in front of them.

"We'll have to break through it," Islaen told them. "Go carefully, though. I don't think it's very deep, and it may end abruptly. We don't want to wind up stumbling over the edge."

Her concern proved well founded. What had appeared at first glance to be a thick miniature forest was in fact a slender curtain of dense growth confined on one side by the perpetual twilight created by the canopy and on the other by the sudden loss of the ground supporting it.

She had been warned both by her map and by Simon himself, but the sight of that drop still left the Colonel cold. Ancient seismic activity and the ceaseless cutting of the fast stream flowing far below had carved out a chasm that seemed to sink a mile or more into the heartstone of the land.

It was not nearly so deep in fact, not half that depth, but the waterway looked no larger than a thread, and she knew it to be a sizable body in reality.

It was also rough and rapid, and it filled the whole floor of the chasm it had carved for itself. Her party would not be able to cross it even if they reached the floor of the deep rift, nor were they likely to successfully scale the opposite wall if they did.

There could be no thought of going down. Those walls were close enough to sheer to make the term reality. It would take proper mountain gear to climb them.

The slit itself was not awesomely wide, but it could not be jumped, and there was no debris lying about nearly long enough to span it, nor would any of the young trees growing in the light it created be able to serve that purpose.

They had two options before them, then, if they were to go on with their mission. They could take on the time-consuming business of bridge building utilizing the various odd-sized pieces of material available to them, or they could use the route the Amazoonan Yeoman had followed. That last would not be a quick process, either, not with four of them, but it should not be quite as bad as the first, and it would be a hair safer. She knew full well that they would not spare themselves the time to make a really good job of any bridge they constructed.

Jake saw the direction of her gaze. "Colonel, has anyone ever mentioned that you're devoid of heart, pity, and mercy?"

The woman smiled. "Frequently, in whole or in part."

"Your mind's made up about going into the treetops?"

"I'm open to other suggestions," she replied seriously, "but it does seem like our best course, Jake."

Their two comrades nodded glumly. Neither was enthusiastic about their proposed route, but they, too, saw the logic of taking it.

Varn strained his eyes to pick out detail in the distance-blurred understory of the canopy. "That branch will be our drop-off point?"

The redhead winced. "That's a poor choice of phrasing, Admiral.—Islaen?"

"Aye, assuming it's as sturdy as it looks. We'll send Bandit up to examine it for us before making the climb."

The limb to which they referred extended far out over the open place, crossed it completely actually, but only in its slender tip. They would be able to utilize only about half of its length, if that much. That had been true for the Amazoonan Yeoman when she had made her own crossing farther south. She had crept out along her chosen branch as far as she had dared and had then swung across the remaining space with the aid of a well-developed vine.

Islaen gave a decisive shake of her head. They need not copy her performance that closely, praise the Spirit of Space. For one thing, there was no guarantee that they would be as fortunate. They might not discover any vines of sufficient length and strength. Even in the luxuriant growth of the jungle world, those capable of meeting their needs had to be at least uncommon, if not actually rarities.

Their own gear would see them through. They had a good coil of rope with them. It was sure and familiar, and all of them could be certain that it would not give way beneath their weight.

The gurry whistled. *Islaen says Bandit can help?*

"Aye, love. You'll fly up and examine that big branch. Link your eyes with Varn's so he can see it, too."

Yes, Islaen!

Bandit whirled skyward, eager to be of service to her companions.

Sogan set his back against a tree. Islaen stepped quickly beside him and laid her hand on his arm to give him a palpable anchor to his actual position. She could not share sight with Bandit directly the way he did, but she knew the melding of their sense receptors could be disruptive, particularly when the Jadite was moving rapidly and irregularly.

The Arcturian braced himself. Sometimes the little hen opened the link abruptly and prematurely in her excitement, to his great discomfort. This time, though, she called out in warning and made a conscious effort to control the speed and motion of her flight, and he did not have to fight too hard to come to terms with the conflicting evidence of body senses and eyes.

The study of the branch required only a few minutes. Sogan praised the gurry, then severed contact with her. When he was certain of his balance once more, he described the place for his comrades.

"It will serve," he concluded. "There is also a second, equally good branch a foot above and less than that to the right of it invisible from here. It would take the rope as well should we decide against the first for any reason." It would also serve as a brace and back rest, he thought to himself. That would not be unwelcome to people perched on what amounted to a slender stick some three hundred fifty feet above the forest floor. His lips tightened. Plus the drop to the river as far again below that.

"We won't climb with the packs," the Commando-Colonel said. 'I'll go up first, then Jake. Once we're secure, we'll haul up the gear. Bethe and Varn can follow after that." She sighed then. "This is not going to be easy."

It was not. Varn Tarl Sogan's arms felt like lead weights as he forced them to keep advancing the rope loop he was using as a climbing belt to support himself as he inched his way up the seemingly interminable length of the great trunk. His legs were trembling with the strain of clasping the wood, of pushing against it. If only he did not give way . . .

The others had made it, even Bethe Danlo. He would do so as well, and under his own power, without relying on the rope dangling comfortingly near. An Arcturian officer could perform at least as well as a Federation spacer.

His vision began to blur, and his breath was coming in wrenching gasps. He had believed himself to be in better condition . . .

His hand struck something. Varn looked numbly at it for a moment, then the life returned to him as if by magic. The branch! He was up!

The war prince quelled his excitement. Not quite. He was still beneath that branch, and getting onto it was not going to be as easy as wishing he were there.

Strong hands closed on his wrists. "Wriggle up, Admiral. I've got you."

With Karmikel's aid, Sogan was soon sitting astride the huge limb, his back resting against the trunk. "Thanks, Jake," he murmured. His eyes closed. The release from effort was an agony in itself.

The others left him alone for a couple of minutes to let him catch his breath, but then he felt Islaen's question brush his mind, and he roused himself. *I am sound out*, he assured her, *more or less*.

His companions were also sitting astride the branch. The former Admiral forgot his dignity for once and slid along the limb until he had joined them. He looked down. Height was no problem for him in itself, and he found the scene awe-inspiring, magnificent as only nature in her great extremes can be.

Magnificent and perilous. "Our rope will do it?" he asked doubtfully.

"Oh, sure," Jake replied. "With lots to spare. We're not trying to reach the river, don't forget, just the other side of the chasm."

"We could even do without it," Islaen Connor added. She leaned forward to slap at a thick wooden vine looped across their branch. "We could just slide down this. It's a vine that made it back to the floor, most conveniently on the other side of the chasm. It's thickened and stiffened into a respectable sapling in its own right, sort of a support trunk for the tree."

"You could slide down it," Bethe interjected. "It's not so big that I'd like to be the last one down following you three and all our baggage."

Karmikel chuckled. "You'll get no argument from me on that score, Sergeant." He glanced at their destination. "I guess there's no point in putting it off any longer."

"No," his commander agreed. "We'll attach the line to the upper branch, I think. It'll be easier taking hold of it from here rather than having to crawl over and climb down to do it."

The demolitions expert nodded her agreement, but she then gave a regretful shake of her head. "It's a pity to lose the rope so soon. It's the longest we have."

"That may not be necessary," Varn told her thoughtfully. "These Amazoonans are a big people. I probably do not weigh much more than that Yeoman and most likely somewhat less. If I remain until last, I could toss down the rope and descend along the vine myself. A single person's traveling it should not put too much strain on it."

"Nice idea, Admiral," the spacer agreed, "but I weigh the least of all of us, so that shot's mine."

"Space will turn white first! While I outrank . . ."

"It's suitability, not rank, that rules on a Commando mission," the blonde told him serenely.

"Quiet, both of you!" Islaen Connor snapped. She thought for several minutes. "I'd like to save the rope. —All right, Varn. It's your idea. You get to carry it."

"But . . ." Bethe protested.

The Colonel shook her head. "If I were enough worried about weight to let that sway me, I wouldn't go for it at all. Besides, he is the stronger of you two, and I want him to handle the baggage, to help steady it if it starts to spin."

Islaen checked the fastening on the rope. She took hold of it without any visible hesitation, but her heart seemed to freeze as she pushed away from her support. The line tightened under her weight, and she clung to it for a moment. This had been an excellent plan in theory. In reality, the fact that only this slim, synthetic strand and insubstantial air stood between her and that raging cataract clouded the logic of the move.

The woman started her descent, using her hands and legs to keep herself from moving too fast. This had to remain a climb, not a slide. Come down too rapidly, and she would not only shred her hands to the bone but would most probably find herself in the river as well with the long climb up to the jungle floor as payment for her carelessness.

That or smashed against a tree. The idea of using this method of descent was to swing across the chasm, not drop into it, but a rope this long could easily sway over far too wide an arc at far too fast a rate, especially with the powerful breeze whipping down the funnel created by the chasm and the tall trees flanking it. If that gained only a little more strength, it would present them with a serious challenge whether they managed the line properly or not.

Whatever its potential hazards, the Commando-Colonel handled her descent well and came to ground at the fringe of the narrow tangle bordering the chasm.

She sighed in relief and started to release the line, but her eyes widened, and her hands froze on it. The breath she had drawn quite literally stopped in her lungs. There on a branch level with her eyes and not four inches from her face was a slender green serpent. It was obviously as thoroughly frightened by her sudden appearance as she was of it. Its triangular head was raised in threat, and its triple tongue darted nervously between its jaws, which were almost certainly armed with sharp fangs designed to inject the potent venom for which such denizens of Amazoon's jungles were justly famed.

There was nothing she could do, no defense she could raise. The creature would strike whether she jumped or remained still, and at this distance, there was no way in all space that it could miss. With her head receiving the full dose, the venom would inevitably prove fatal, probably in a matter of moments.

Varn!

The scream broke from her before her will could raise shields to block it. In the next instant the Arcturian's mind was with her. She could feel the call, the command, pouring out from him, reassuring the snake that she represented no threat to it and ordering it to withdraw.

Several fraction-seconds passed, then the lovely, deadly creature lowered its head and seemed to flow back along the branch to disappear into the mass of vegetation behind it.

Islaen held on to the rope as her legs seemed to turn to water. *Thanks, Admiral. I owe you that one.*

My pleasure to be of some use, Colonel.

His thoughts stayed with her until she was enough herself to release the line again, then he withdrew and began scanning their surroundings for any more unwelcome wildlife. Even after failing to uncover anything himself, he sent Bandit down to continue the search. The ill luck of a fall would have to be borne should that happen, but he would not permit any of his comrades to be lost through this other cause.

Jake made it down and then Bethe, neither experiencing any difficulty or trouble apart from the basic hardship of the descent. Sogan lowered their packs two at a time. These proved harder to manage than he had anticipated. Their lighter weight rendered them more vulnerable than his comrades had been to the buffeting of the wind, and it required some skilled playing on his part to set them where he wanted.

The last bundle was on the ground. He called to Islaen to give her time to secure her end of the rope lest it otherwise be pulled into the chasm, waited a couple of seconds, then released it from the high branch. It slithered by him, slapped against the living wood, and was gone.

We got it, Varn! Islaen told him moments later. *Come on down yourself.*

The former Admiral maneuvered himself along the tree limb until he came to the hardened vine that was to be his road. His heart speeded unpleasantly as his fingers curled over it.

There was no help for it. He turned, and grasping the branch on either side of it tightly, he gingerly lowered himself, clutching at the seemingly impossibly slender vine with his legs. His eyes shut. It did not help, physically or psychologically, that he could not as yet see it.

It required an act of will to dislodge first one hand and then the other from the solid branch and transfer them to the slight thing to which he clung, but that, too, he accomplished without delay. If he stopped or thought too long about it, he might freeze.

That was actually the worst of it, as Sogan had known it would be, barring accident. Once fully on the vine and moving, he made good progress. It was not an enjoyable journey, but it was safe enough despite his dislike of it, and it was easier than his comrades' descent had been. He was coming down on an incline with reasonable support under him, sparing his muscles the strain of carrying his whole weight.

His greatest difficulty was in controlling his speed. This was a slide in fact, and too rapid movement caused his slender support to vibrate and whip beneath him until he feared it would snap altogether, break away with him still clinging to it.

Varn managed to bring himself to a stop and clutched the vine almost convulsively while one particularly violent series of spasms spent themselves. He cursed himself roundly for proposing this ridiculous plan. They could have need of that rope later, and the idea had seemed imminently reasonable in theory, but he should have realized that putting it into practice would be another matter.

Varn?

He started and began to slam his shields into place, but he realized in time that the Colonel was still ashamed of her earlier fear and cry for help, and he allowed her to see his less reasonably founded discomfort. *There is nothing wrong*, he assured her in the next instant. *My road is somewhat unstable, and I wanted to let it grow still again before continuing.*

Smart move, she agreed. *Take your time, Varn. You're doing fine.*

If he took his time, he would be hanging between ground and sky for the next two weeks, the man thought miserably, but he made himself start downward again. To make matters worse, he was now plaguey hot once more. If nothing else, it had at least been reasonably cool up there among the branches.

The final twenty feet proved to be a nasty shock. The vine had plunged straight into the ground from there, at an angle absolutely perpendicular to it. He faced more of a drop than a climb.

Slogan braked himself as best he could and managed to come to ground smoothly enough that he was able to face his comrades with a show of triumph.

The demolitions expert glowered at him. "That didn't look half bad, Admiral," she accused. "The last part might almost have been fun. I think you knew it'd be a nice assignment and decided to keep it for yourself."

"The prerogatives of rank, Sergeant," he told her archly.

He felt Islaen's laugh ring in his thoughts, but the biting retort in his own tongue came only because she anticipated it. It was good to hear laughter from her following so soon upon her own scare, even if he was the butt of it.

Their fingers brushed lightly, then they retrieved their packs while their comrades recoiled the rope, and the four Commandos set out once more.

EIGHT

ISLAEN CONNOR CHECKED her map against her latest compass reading before restoring both to her utility belt. She did so with no good humor. Another barrier, supposedly not a bad one, lay ahead, but the Spirit ruling space knew, she did not want to face any more challenges today. What she really wanted was to wake up cool and comfortable in her bunk on the *Fairest Maid* or in their chamber on Thorne with Varn's arms around her.

She would have to finish this business before either was going to happen, she thought glumly as she signaled a halt. Their next problem was before them.

They cut their way through the inevitable shrub thicket to the rim of another rift in the ground. This was neither as deep nor anything as broad as the first had been. They could almost have jumped it, but the Colonel would not consider making the attempt. Near thing as it was, the distance was simply too great even had there been a clear landing place on the opposite bank instead of another wall of undergrowth.

They could climb this one, but a quicker, physically easier solution was readily at hand. "Fell some of these saplings," she ordered. "Three will do. We'll lash them together and walk over."

Her comrades were quick to obey, and soon they had a narrow but serviceable footbridge thrown across the crevasse.

Islaen shifted her pack for maximum comfort and balance. They would take their baggage over with them this time. "We'll do it one at a time and go roped. There's no point in taking needless chances."

She did not hurry the crossing, short as it was. The

makeshift bridge was narrow, and her burden was unwieldy enough to threaten her balance should she step off center only a fraction.

It was over at last. Jake and Bethe took their time as well, especially the former, who was struggling under the pull of the bulky boat, but they, too, reached their destination in good order.

The war prince prepared to take his turn. He fastened the rope about himself, then signaled to his companions that he was set.

His first tentative steps confirmed the care a successful crossing would require, but his spacer's balance asserted itself, and he felt confident enough to touch his mind with his consort's. *It would not have hurt to cut another sapling, Colonel*, he grumbled. *I shall not be pleased if I have to be hauled out of that hole like some prize fish.*

She smiled, knowing he would not be talking like this, be talking at all, if he were having trouble. *Never mind the complaints, Admiral. I ran precisely the same risk myself.*

I do not think you would have looked quite as amusing in that situation, Colonel Connor.

She laughed but still held her breath until he had made it over. "Onward, Comrades," she said then. "The next stop's the river."

Aye, she thought, but they would not reach it without a battle. Unlike the thin screen of undergrowth walling the two crevasses, the tangle following the course of the Maiden, of any major waterway, was broad and immeasurably more difficult to penetrate. They would be well spent before they got any glimpse of the stream that was to be their highway for the next leg of their trek.

Jake Karmikel rubbed a wet sleeve across his forehead to keep any more sweat from dripping into his eyes. He hoped viciously that he had managed to wipe out at least a million of the tiny dark things buzzing incessantly around and on his head, hood, and skin alike. His face was as speckled as if he had the Surian Spot, each red dot the mark of a successful attack by some minute—or occasionally not so small—flier, and he felt no friendliness toward any of their kind.

He laughed bitterly to himself. Kill a million of them? That would not even dent this thrice-blasted host!

The Noreenan breathed deeply. It had taken them an hour to cut through the tangle, an hour to cover a space that he should have been able to cross in five minutes had it been anything approaching normal ground. He had borne the brunt of it as well. He was physically the strongest of the party, and his comrades, with enforced practicality of their kind, had assigned him to the point for the duration.

They were through it now, at least, and the river, the Maiden, rolled before them.

It was not an encouraging sight. They all knew a rough course when they saw one, and that waterway looked scarcely easier to negotiate than the approach to it had been.

The debris of every sort that it carried showed the pattern of its flow all too clearly. Pattern? The Maiden was not so much a united force as a loose alliance of sometimes conflicting and always irritable currents under only tentative control by the powerful central stream. Navigating on that was not going to be any pleasure jaunt.

Use it, they must, the Commando-Captain thought wearily as he set his pack down and detached the inflatable boat from it. With his comrades' aid, he carefully unfolded the boat and removed two small cylinders of gas from the self-envelope on what would become the inner portion of her prow.

She was an ingenious invention, Jake had to admit. When this small amount of the two compounds united, they formed a third, a gas that multiplied itself until it filled all the space within the walls of the portable craft. Moreover, another chemical was set at intervals within those walls that reacted with the gas to create a thick, impermeable membrane, thereby dividing the whole of the vessel into a series of separate compartments. If one or more were punctured, the others would still sustain her. Even if a whole side went out, the passengers could still cling to the other. Of course, in some sections of these rivers, those where sawmills swam, that would only momentarily prolong a very agonizing inevitable end.

He screwed the cover off the first cylinder. The second resisted him. He applied more pressure, then swore when it still refused to give.

Islaen turned, alerted as much by what he was transmitting as by the sharpness of his words. "Problems, Jake?"

"Damn thing won't open."

The Arcturian was kneeling beside the boat. He looked up. "I cannot get to the inlet valve, either. The heat of the fire seems to have fused the protective covering."

"We'll never get the other one going if that's the case," Bethe Danlo told them. "That took an even worse toasting."

"Do your best, Comrades," their commander advised. "If the boats won't work out, we'll have a lot of wood to chop. —Come on, Bethe. Let's leave them at it and get this gear set up for the voyage."

Jake looked from the container in his hand to his companion. "Did you Arcturians believe in jinxed missions, Admiral?"

"No. Not officially."

"Unofficially?"

"We took great care never to mention the subject, at least not until the assignment in question was long over."

Karmikel chuckled. "For two peoples so widely separated, we seem to share a lot of the same good ideas."

The men worked in silence for some minutes, then the Noreenan gave a crow of triumph.

Sogan glanced at him. "Success?"

"Aye. —How're you coming?"

"It is loosening. I should have it in another couple of minutes."

It was late in the day already, and Islaen ordered that they break off their labors as soon as they confirmed that they would be able to inflate the boat baring further complications. The journey downriver was not going to be an easy one, even if its problems would be of a different nature from those they had encountered thus far. It would be best to be as rested as possible when they set out on it.

NINE

THE FOUR COMPLETED their preparations for the next stage of their mission with the first light. The boat inflated without difficulty, and Islaen Connor studied her with satisfaction. She was a trim-looking little craft and bigger than any of them had imagined she would be. It would still unquestionably be a tight fit, but the boat would hold all four of them plus their gear.

Her eyes flickered to her consort, who was helping the redhead stow the spare boat. "Varn, when you're finished there, will you refill the canteens?" she asked, speaking aloud for the benefit of their comrades. "The rest of us'll get the remainder of this stuff on board."

"Sure thing, Colonel. We are done here now."

"Good. —Bandit, you go along and take care of him."

Yes, Islaen!

Sogan smiled to himself as he collected the canteens and moved away from the others. The gurry had been flitting from one member of the team to the other and sending out a constant stream of comments and questions in her excitement over the seemingly magical inflation of the boat and the prospect of the river journey. Islaen had not thought he needed protecting. She had wanted to secure a few minutes' peace for herself.

All the canteens were light. They had been forced to drink heavily with the sweat they were losing in order to maintain their bodies' fluid balance. It was fortunate a good replacement supply was near at hand.

He pushed his way through the wall of plants along the water's edge until he found a spot where a slight bend created a comparatively gentle pool where he would be able to fill the narrow-mouthed vessels without chancing having one of them swept out of his hands by the full current.

He crouched down, sighing at the cloud of annoyed insects roused out of the disturbed vegetation. They would be even worse when he was down on his belly hanging over the water, he thought, and with his hands full, he would not even be able to slap at them.

The Arcturian peered into the pool. It was deep enough but clear to the bottom in the manner of most highland waters. They would purify it as a precaution, but there was probably no real need to do so.

Despite the uncommonly heavy recent rains, the Maiden did not completely fill its channel, and the bank rose well above its surface. Varn stretched out full length on his stomach but still could not reach the water to fill the canteens. He would have to work his way down a bit.

He started to squirm forward.

Varn, stop! Nooo!

The gurry streaked in front of him, so close that the tip of her wing almost clipped his eyes. She dove straight for the water, swooping up again just as she seemed about to plunge into the river.

She did not come up alone. Sogan felt her captive before he saw the thing, a long, thread-thin, nearly transparent creature thrashing madly in her bill.

He shuddered. A spring leech. Had she not seen it . . .

His throat closed. That blood sucker could fatally drain a being as small as Bandit in a matter of minutes, and even as he recognized the danger to her, its fear and anger changed to anticipation.

It tensed, readied itself to fling its wirelike body through the open slit of the bill grasping it.

Desperately, he drove the thought, the concept, of poison into the leech. For a minute part of a second, the tension stiffening its body held, then it drooped and squirmed in an effort to break free.

"Bandit, drop it!" he shouted. "Let it go, small one!" His ruse would not hold long against instinct.

The gurry obeyed, returning her captive to its domain. Whistling with satisfaction, she flew to him and nestled in the hand he cupped to receive her. *It's all right, Varn! Bandit got rid of the spring leech.*

He only stroked her, too relieved to speak either with voice or mind. Had he failed to influence the creature, had she been less quick in obeying his order, the leech would almost certainly have succeeded in attaching itself. What would he have done then? How could he have freed her of it in time?

Varn, where are you? What's wrong?

His head snapped up, and he belatedly realized the intensity of the fear he had been broadcasting. *Here, Islaen. Everything is all right now.*

The Commando-Colonel broke through the brush, her blaster at ready and set to slay. She came to a dead stop. Her eyes fixed on Bandit, on the way he was holding her clutched to his breast. "Spirit of Space," she whispered aloud. *What's happened to her?*

The gurry stopped her purring in complete surprise. *Nothing's wrong, Islaen! Bandit helped Varn, just like you said!*

Bethe and Jake joined them in that moment, both of them fully armed. They holstered their weapons when they saw nothing amiss.

"What's going on, Sogan?" Karmikel demanded gruffly. Islaen had been really spooked by the sending she had received. That meant that the former Admiral had also had a bad scare or experience of some sort.

Tersely, Varn described what had happened. "I never saw the thing," he concluded. "It would have been down my throat if it had not been for Bandit."

Leech invisible! the Jadite said in his defense.

"Transparent," he corrected automatically, forgetting that only the Noreenan woman had heard her.

"Couldn't you feel it?" Bethe Danlo asked him.

He shook his head. "I probably did, but there were so many things around hungering for my blood that it was all a blur."

His mouth hardened. "I let myself forget about those things, and Bandit was nearly killed as a result."

Jake shook his head sharply. "Their camouflage is excellent, and spring leeches prey successfully on creatures bred with them on this steam pit of a planet."

"If anyone's at fault, it's me," Islaen Connor said, silencing them both. "I broke one of the cardinal rules of our profession and let one of the unit go off alone unnecessarily in country like this."

Bandit was with Varn! she protested.

"I know you were, love. We can be thankful you were, but he might have met with a human enemy, and he should've had a human comrade to back him. You should not be expected to fight our wars for us."

"That's past," the demolitions expert told them impatiently. "The question is, what now? Those horrors are in every stream and pool on Amazoon where there's anyplace for them to anchor and it's not too deep or too far out for them to have a crack at potential victims. We'll have a delightful time trying to collect water."

"We'll wear masks," the Colonel answered, "over both face and mouth. Goggles, too. They're not supposed to go for eyes, but we're not taking any more chances, not with anything we can avoid or counter. —Now, let's move before something else happens. We've wasted more than enough time around here as it is."

TEN

VARN TARL SOGAN remained withdrawn, his thoughts closed and subdued, but the Maiden gave him little opportunity to sink into guilt. The launching and boarding were easily accomplished, but they had not pulled more than six feet out from the bank before a vicious side current ripped into them. All four struggled to hold their unfamiliar craft steady and under their control, while Sogan, who had command of her, fought to edge her into midstream.

After several uncertain minutes, he succeeded. Almost immediately, some of the tension left him. He had read this right, at least. The main current was powerful enough to resist most of the turmoil boiling on either side, sometimes easing, sometimes growing violent as a smaller river or stream joined with the Maiden. It was also strong enough and fast enough to carry the light boat, relieving the guerrillas of the need to power her advance themselves.

Although free of what could have been a heavy, unremitting chore, they enjoyed no easy ride. The oars and poles rarely left their hands. They had to battle to maintain their position despite the strength of the main stream, and constant vigilance was needed to keep the vessel away from potential hazards. The river was nowhere a very deep waterway, and boulders and projecting logs were a perpetual threat to any craft venturing on its surface.

So, too, were many of the things swept along by the current. Although the off-worlders knew their boat was tough and that the material out of which she had been fashioned was designed

64

to withstand conditions on Amazoon's waters, it was impossible for them to forget that she was only an inflatable emergency craft intended for brief use during a survival situation, not for a long, deliberate trek to a military target. Some of the debris floating and swirling beside her looked to be as heavy as she was, and much of it bristled with sharp projections. It moved fast and rather unexpectedly at times, as well, and they had to keep constantly at ready to fend off any such missiles before they struck and perhaps holed her.

The rain fell again as it had on the previous day, a heavy, sullen shower that failed to scrub any of the humidity out of the air. It halved visibility, but they welcomed it all the same. If it was of no benefit long-term, the downpour was at least cool in itself and the first relief they had known from the choking heat since they had descended from the treetops.

It was still coming down steadily when Islaen's brows drew together. Her frown deepened as she listened intently for several seconds. *Varn, do you hear something? The river sounds different.*

No. —Aye, you are right. I do. It is far ahead yet, I think.

He strained his eyes, trying to peer through the wall of falling water. There were many rapids and small falls along the Maiden's course, and it would be deadly to come upon one of them without some real warning.

Bandit will scout! She'll let Varn see!

Without waiting for the humans' leave, she took wing and streaked downriver, quickly vanishing from their sight.

The Arcturian braced himself, but he still swayed and clutched the railing when the gurry's sight and sound receptors suddenly opened into his, swamping him with a flood of conflicting sensory stimuli. He hastily shut his eyes so that his mind had to deal only with the information the Jadite was sending to him, but even so, he had to battle his other senses, which gave very different testimony from that which his vision now reported, that and the effects of Bandit's flight, which he now seemed to experience, and the simultaneous motion of the boat.

All that, he had anticipated, and in a few moments, he had brought enough order to the tumble of impressions flowing into him that he was able to give his attention to the scene seemingly before and below him.

It was grim enough, a stretch of seething, furious water racing down a two-mile-long, steep slide through the impossibly narrow channels created by the veritable forest of boulders filling all that part of the riverbed.

Sogan remained with the gurry for about five minutes, then he thanked her and withdrew from the link.

The return was not as unsettling a business, but he still welcomed the continuing support of Islaen's slender, steadying arm until his perceptions had regained their normal focus.

At last, he straightened and nodded to indicate that he was himself once more.

Bethe Danlo's slate-blue eyes were on him. "It doesn't get any easier, does it?" she asked sympathetically. The war prince had really looked ill this time.

"Being in this boat did not help," Varn admitted with a wry smile.

He shrugged. That was past and quite irrelevant. He ordered his companions to brace their vessel with the poles to hold her in place while he reported what he had learned.

"How long do we have before we hit rough water?" the Colonel asked when he had finished.

"About twenty minutes. The river is both growing shallower and picking up speed and fall. That is the difference you detected. The change in its flow has altered its sound as well."

"You're a damn sight more observant than the rest of us, Colonel." Jake was open in his admiration, but he turned back to the second man almost before he had finished speaking. "You're our water expert, Admiral. What do you suggest we do when we get there?"

"Ride it out, of course."

Karmikel stared at him. Sogan's expression did not change until the women could no longer control their laughter, then he grinned broadly at the Noreenan's discomfort. "We shall have to work our way around it."

"You're a son of a Scythian ape, Varn Tarl Sogan," Jake growled without malice. The answer had been so obvious that he had fully deserved to get run over the jets for ever raising the question. "How about being a bit more specific, or haven't you quite worked that part of it out yet?"

"Do we carry everything overland?" the Commando-Sergeant interjected unenthusiastically.

To her relief, Varn shook his head. "The tangle is too heavy on most of both banks. There is a channel along the left, chiefly the work of a couple of side currents. It will not be easy, but we should be able to bring her through."

The other three nodded their understanding as he described their proposed route in greater detail.

"We should be able to manage it," Islaen agreed. She sighed to herself. Strenuous physical labor was not the aspect of her profession that she cherished most, and the only way they were going to get their vessel through that place was to get out and push and drag her.

Sogan confirmed that in the next moment. "I will guide. The rest of you shall have to take to the ropes."

"There seems to be a certain inequity in that duty roster," Jake complained.

The Arcturian's dark eyes sparkled. "As you yourself said, friend, I am our water expert. Therefore, the delicate task of steering must naturally fall to me."

A whistle sounding in both his mind and ears caused him to look up as the gurry hen flew out of the gray wall of rain and perched on the railing beside him.

Bandit helped? Varn knows what to do now?

"Aye to both questions, small one. You did well for all of us."

"She's soaked!" Bethe exclaimed. "Come over here, pet. I can be drying you off while we're talking."

Bandit's fine! she protested, but she complied and submitted herself to the spacer's ministrations with every sign of pleasure.

The softness that gentled the former Admiral's usually stern features while he watched the little Jadite faded as he turned once more to the task at hand. "We might as well get moving, Comrades. The Maiden is not going to grow quiet for our benefit."

Islaen Connor swore under her breath as her foot slipped yet again on the smooth-worn rocks littering the riverbed. If it had not been for the support of the strong, high boots, she would have twisted an ankle, or both of them, long before now.

She and Bethe were on either side of the Amazoonan craft, hauling on the short ropes they were using to pull her. Jake Karmikel pushed from behind where his muscle could be put to the best use.

Varn remained aboard, but his job was scarcely less strenuous than the others'. He not only had the responsibility of guiding the boat and directing the efforts of his comrades, but time after time, he had to throw his weight against the long pole to force the undermanned vessel away from some obstruction or from the never-distant bank.

Whatever about that, it went ill with him to see Islaen Connor up to her waist and sometimes her breasts in water, her shoulders bent and straining against that rope, while he rode dry.

The Noreenan woman knew he was unhappy with the arrangement reason had made him propose and masked as much as she could of the various discomforts and mishaps she endured, completely screening any pain she felt. It was minor anyway, and she could not see adding more fuel to his discontent.

There were even some advantages to her position. The rain had stopped at last, leaving behind it an atmosphere saturated with moisture and a heat to which there seemed no end. The water was at least cooling, and few of the river's living dangers were to be encountered in a rough stretch like this. Their clothing provided sufficient defense against those. Fortunately, spring leeches were not among them, and so they were able to work unmasked.

She gasped as her calf slammed against the sharp end of an embedded branch or trunk of a young sapling. Damn her carelessness! *Sorry, Varn,* she said, knowing he had felt something of that jab. Like a fool, she had forgotten herself and had been traveling loosely shielded when it happened.

Are you all right?

Sound out apart from what I suppose'll be a planet-sized bruise. It's no more than I deserve for collecting stardust instead of watching where I was going.

You are tiring. Change places with me for a while . . .

When space turns white, Admiral! You're serving us best right where you are. —How's Bandit doing?

He frowned. *Do not try to manipulate me, Islaen.*

I'm not. I'm just changing a totally unprofitable subject. Her brown eyes shadowed. *She really got soaked. There's not much chance of taking a chill, but there's almost no drying in this humidity. If a fungus or mold gets into her feathers or on her skin, we'll have a stellar time . . .*

The man laughed. *Your maternal instincts are flaring up, Colonel Connor. —Bethe did a thorough job drying her, and Bandit took care of any remaining dampness very efficiently. She is nice and snug right here under the edge of the tarp where she can keep an eye on me.*

Yes, Islaen! Bandit's fine! Only too hot! Thorne's nicer!

Aye, Bandit, the woman agreed wearily. *Right now, I wouldn't mind being there myself.*

Sogan was quiet for a few moments. When he did speak again, he did not attempt to screen his concern. *Islaen, I am worried about Bethe. She is small for such work. Even you have a good six inches on her, and this channel deepens considerably in places, sometimes with very little warning.*

The Commando-Colonel acknowledged that with a slow nod. *I know. She's gone to her chin a couple of times.* The demolitions expert could swim—they all could—but the current was bad. If she lost her footing and could not get herself in control almost immediately, she could be swept out into the main stream and the turmoil of the rapids.

Islaen sighed. They needed to keep that rope manned. *She's careful. As long as fortune doesn't sling us any nasty shots, she should be all right, or at no worse risk than the rest of us.*

Fortune has fired more than one projectile at us on this one, he reminded her gloomily.

The woman shot him a quick, sharp look. Varn Tarl Sogan had called a bad mission correctly before, often enough that she suspected the ability to do so, at least partially, came from as yet another aspect of his mind talent and not merely from his well-honed warrior's senses.

Sogan read her question and shook his head emphatically physically and in thought. That was one gift he was not willing to acknowledge, not unless and until it was unequivocally proven that he did in fact possess it. The mere fact of his mutation was difficult enough to accept, to bear, for one of a race that loathed significant alteration from their prototype standard. He used and was grateful for the aid of the strange powers he possessed, but even now, he rarely permitted himself to dwell on them. He found it well-nigh unendurable even to consider that he might also be able, however hazily, to peer a space into the future.

ELEVEN

IT WAS A long two miles, but they reached the end of the rapids at last, and Varn helped his sopping wet comrades back on board, where they immediately turned their efforts to guiding their vessel back out into the center of the once more relatively mild Maiden.

Only then could they sit back and truly relax for a few minutes. Bethe Danlo's eyes closed as she flexed her arms and shoulders in an effort to work the weariness out of them. "Bandit was right," she muttered to her commander. "We should all have stayed home."

Yes! the gurry agreed. *Poor Bethe's tired!*

"Poor Jake and poor Islaen are just as tired," the Colonel told her, drawing a laugh from the others.

"I guess she thinks you two are hardier," the spacer commented. "There's no hope that this was our last such haul, I suppose?"

"None," Sogan said. "Both the maps and Salombo's descriptions agree on that. We are just fortunate that this is not the flood season, or we would be facing a lot more of the same. As it is, there will probably be just one more block, but it is a major one."

"I know," she said glumly. "I was there, too, when Simon described it. I was just hoping to hear you contradict all that."

She nibbled absently at the ration packet the former Admiral handed her after quick-frying it on his plutonium disk. "Actually, it wouldn't be half bad if the riverbed were in any way clean, but there're rocks everywhere, and every one of them's damn near as smooth as fine marble. Even our service boots can't get much purchase on them."

"Bare feet would probably work better," her husband agreed slowly.

Bethe stared at him. "With all the wriggly things in that water, not to mention the extraneous sharp objects? Have you got your brain stored where you keep your credits?"

"Just a suggestion, Sergeant," he informed her archly. "I wasn't contemplating trying it myself."

"I'll put credits down that you weren't, you big asteroid!" she said sourly.

Islaen laughed. "Easy on the drive, my friends. You'll be needing that energy for other things quite soon enough."

The Commando-Colonel's prediction proved all too accurate. Far too quickly for any of them, the Maiden began to give warning of trouble ahead for those able to read her signals. The surface literally foamed as the water swirled and darted, first in one direction, then in another. The banks on either side looked dark and ominous; the sharp, biting wavelets had dug far into the soft soil, gnawing out holes that in some spots of particularly intense activity qualified for the name of caves. The whole length, even where it had suffered the lightest damage, was deeply undercut. Above all was a rumbling that grew even louder and more threatening.

The angrily pitching boat rounded a sharp bend, and the reason behind the roiled water, the source of the incessant roar, was there before them.

Bethe Danlo felt her mouth go dry. All the center of the river fell away into a waterfall. It was only some twelve feet high, but the drop was absolutely sheer, and an immense, wicked-looking whirlpool swirled at its base.

The left channel was fairly large, but it was completely sealed off as far as their boat was concerned. A neat row of boulders trapped much of the larger debris striking against it, building a veritable wall of logs, branches, and brush that grew ever larger and more formidable until the floods of the rainy season tore it down again. There would be no going through that way.

The right side was little more promising, just a single, narrow flow that was a full rapid in its own right rumbling along dangerously close to the main torrent. A partly submerged spur of gravel and other matter backed up behind a great, flat-faced rock separated it from the rest of the river.

She glanced first at the Colonel, then at Varn Tarl Sogan. They would have to move, and move now, whatever they decided to do.

The same chill touched the former Admiral's heart, but he realized even at that first glance that they had but one course open to them. It would not be possible even to pull out on one of the overgrown banks at this point and cut their way down to the bottom. He gave the order to take her to the right.

Once in the somewhat quieter side stream, they had to take to the water again. All four of them went over the side this time. In that confined space and sharp current, there was no need for anyone to remain aboard; the boat had nowhere to go but ahead provided they kept her under tight rein.

Once more, the Colonel and Sergeant pulled, but they used only one rope with Islaen in the lead and Bethe behind her. Their male comrades had the task of pushing from behind and that of moving along one side or the other to clear away rocks or gravel impeding their vessel's progress.

It was not easy work, particularly for the spacer, who was forced to move shoulder deep most of the time. The current pushing them on was strong and was tiring in itself, and it had a subtle but compelling pull toward the left that made it necessary to fight the boat the whole of the way. If once she grounded on the gravel bar, it would be difficult or perhaps impossible to release her again.

They had traveled nearly three quarters of the way to the falls when suddenly Bethe slid on a smooth, loosely embedded stone, and her legs went out from under her. Her arms flailed in an instinctive effort to right herself, and in the instant she released the rope, the current had her.

"Islaen!"

Even before the stark terror of finding herself so held and helpless forced that cry from her, Islaen Connor had felt the Sergeant's distress. Giving the rope three quick twists around her left arm to anchor herself, she threw herself into the other woman's path.

Their bodies touched. The Noreenan grasped for a hold, caught one of Bethe's hands. The small, cold fingers twined with hers.

For a moment Islaen thought they were away with it, then her friend's hand began to slip. Their flesh was wet and slick, their senses partly numbed by immersion and chill, their muscles stiff and weary after the heavy, close work on the rope, and she realized with an infinite horror that they would not be able to maintain their grasp.

Desperately she tried to bring her left arm to bear in time. Two seconds, three, went by as their hands slowly pulled apart. Bethe's fingers tightened convulsively, then straightened and slid away from hers.

"Bethe! The Spirit of Space help us, I've lost her!"

The Colonel was not aware she had cried out as she watched the blond woman pulled downriver. For the space of a breath, Bethe remained on the surface, then she was sucked under.

The spacer resurfaced as she passed over the gravel spit and managed to keep afloat in the torrent beyond, but there was no resisting the surging drive of the river. She was rushed to the lip of the falls, and she was gone.

Varn Tarl Sogan's head snapped up at the demolitions expert's single, terrified call.

Islaen's triumph and nearly instantaneous defeat followed fast upon it.

"Stay with the boat!" he commanded as he leaped for the rear of the vessel. In that moment both he and Jake heard the Colonel's cry of loss.

Trusting to speed and his spacer's balance to keep him on his feet, the off-worlder raced the length of the boat, reaching her prow as Bethe Danlo went over the falls.

Scarcely pausing to collect himself, he plunged into the stream. The Arcturian swam with it, using the current to add power to his own strong strokes until he reached the great rock anchoring the gravel bar. This stood firm against all pressure. He clung to it, then raised himself upon it until he could look down over the edge of the falls.

His eyes closed momentarily in sheer relief. Bethe lived. She had somehow managed to avoid the chaos at the base of the drop, and she was now fighting to escape the hold of the whirlpool created by the falls.

His joy was short-lived. The situation was still desperate. The spacer was trapped, unable to break out of the water's hold, and very soon now, her strength would fail or she would be smashed against one of the many huge rocks littering the place.

Her cause was not lost. Another approach could win her free . . .

There was no point in trying to shout directions to her. Between the roar of the falls and her own efforts, she simply would not be able to hear and piece together enough of what he said to guide her out of her peril, even if her muscles and skill were equal to the task.

Once more, Sogan dove into the Maiden, into the place where the river surged over the edge of the hard rock shelf forming the falls.

His was a studied descent. He did not crash down the major face of the cascade as Bethe Danlo had done. Rather, he slithered along the channel where they intended to bring their boat. Varn went down fast despite his efforts to check his fall, but he kept control of himself, squirming his supple body around boulders and other obstructions so that he took no real hurt, and he hit bottom before fear had time to build into a significant force inside him.

It was impossible to remain on the surface in that place of impact, and he made no effort to do so. The war prince went under, riding with instead of fighting the command of the Maiden, all the way to the bottom of the deep trench excavated by the eternal pulverizing force of the falling water.

The fear that had held off earlier began to grip him now so that he had to battle himself to keep it from taking control of him. The pressure of the dropping water and the currents it engendered were both worse than he had anticipated. Getting away from this place into which he had cast himself would be no simple matter.

The fall itself was a veritable wall because of the force and volume of the water involved. He could not pierce it. Worse, instead of turning outward when it struck bottom, the whole of it spun inward until it hit hard against the cliff and from thence shot upward, fashioning a vicious trap for a swimmer unfortunate enough to find himself within it.

Once again, the war prince did not attempt to fight the river directly, knowing any such effort to be foredoomed. He worked his way diagonally through it, wielding his will with iron force to control his lungs' ever-more-urgent demand for air.

He tried to figure out how Bethe had made her escape, what route she might have taken and the method she had used to gain it, but he gave the effort up even as he began it. The Commando-Sergeant had never been here. She had either jumped or been thrown out beyond the foot of the falls, or she would not now be alive and still fighting for her survival.

He went on grimly. All this water had to be exiting somewhere, making way for that coming after it, and the sweep of the outlet current was probably no minor power in its own right. It should be able to help him considerably if he could manage to position himself correctly within it.

To do that, he must first find it—before his hold over his lungs gave out and before he was struck by some debris missile tearing down from above . . .

The pressure pushing at him eased suddenly, almost too suddenly, but he identified the cause in time to benefit from it. The outflow was surprisingly gentle, but he followed it. When the turmoil lessened perceptibly, he surfaced to find himself in the quiet main pool of the waterfall.

Once his lungs' hunger for air had been satisfied, Sogan shook his head to clear some of the water from his hair and eyes. He saw his quarry almost at once. She was clinging to a tall, smooth-worn tooth of stone rising out of the wild water near the whirlpool's inner edge.

The woman, in her turn, felt a surge of joy at the sight of him. She had been certain he would never win free, that the falls would be his death.

Whatever her relief, she did not lose her head. There was no sense in both of them dying here. "Varn, head for shore!" she shouted. "There's no getting to me! You can make it to land from where you are."

"Not a chance, Sergeant!"

The Arcturian swam as close as he dared to her without

falling into the grasp of the fierce current pummeling the tall stone.

He could reach her, he decided after several minutes' close study, but not without enormous effort and a great deal more good luck than Bethe Danlo had enjoyed thus far. It was as much as he could manage to hold himself in place even in this comparatively still spot.

There was another way. "Give me your hand if you can," he told her. "I will try to pull you free."

Bethe bit her lip when she looked at the distance separating them, but she tightened her grip on her support with one arm and extended the other to him.

Varn stretched as far as he could in an effort to grasp that pathetically tiny hand, but the space between them was too great. He could not reach her without venturing himself into the swirling maelstrom battering at her refuge.

A feeling of hopelessness all but overwhelmed him. Once in there, it would take his full strength just to keep afloat and battle his own way out again. He would be of no use whatsoever to his comrade.

He treaded water, thinking. The answer came suddenly, so simple that he cursed himself for having overlooked it for so long. If it would work.

"Bethe, hold on with both hands. Tightly. Stretch your body full length toward me."

Again, the spacer silenced her doubts and her fear. It took her several seconds to comply, but at last, she lay outstretched on the surface like a pennant in a stiff wind.

She still seemed so far.

Varn Tarl Sogan would not allow himself to abandon hope. He filled his lungs deeply and dived for the slightly quieter water beneath the surface. A few powerful strokes brought him to the current he had to avoid. He came up just outside it and, treading water again, reached toward her as far as he could. His fingers touched leather and closed on a booted foot.

"Let go, Bethe! I have you!"

The woman released the stone. Immediately the current struck her hard, endeavoring to sweep her up and rip her out of his hold.

Sogan swam for the gentle haven beyond. If he was not

strong enough, or if her foot pulled loose from that boot, she was lost.

Bethe Danlo fought with him for her life, battling the river, relieving him as much as possible of that need so that he could concentrate on pulling her, pulling them both, out of the current's grasp. For what seemed like infinite hours, they struggled against the seemingly consciously relentless hold of the water, then they were floating free in the calm of the big pool below the chaos of the falls.

The spacer righted herself. Her arms closed around Varn in the tight grip of panic, but she quickly regained control again with a discipline born more of a lifetime spent facing the demands of space than of her more recent military training. She allowed the war prince to half tow, half guide her as they drew away from the waterfall's domain and angled toward the damp but wonderfully solid surface of the bank.

TWELVE

IT TOOK THE command of her will, but Islaen Connor submitted herself to the rule she and her consort had set upon themselves almost from their discovery of the talent they shared, that of holding their minds apart from each other in moments of physical crisis lest one or both of them be distracted at the wrong moment with disastrous result.

She had work enough of her own to keep her occupied. The boat still had to be brought down, and with only two of them to handle the job, she was almost unmanageable.

Her eyes closed when a quiet eddy gave her a few moments in which she might rest. Rest and think. Fear was a screaming siren within her. She wanted nothing more than to go down to Varn, to aid him, or failing that, to at least be able to watch his progress.

Her hands did not loosen on the rope. She could not leave this job. Not only was the on-world craft and the supplies she carried necessary to their mission, but she could too easily become a deadly missile if she broke free now and plunged over the falls. Their comrades fighting for their lives below would have little hope of surviving if she careened down on top of them.

Jake's anguish equaled her own. Islaen might not dare to contact the war prince at this stage, but she was wide open to Karmikel's transmissions and could feel the full measure of his misery, the bitter weight of his fear, and the sense of impotence because he could give no direct help to his wife. Any doubt she might have had about the strength and depth of his feeling for Bethe Danlo faded in that moment. He loved the Sergeant, and he was paying the full price for that love in this time of her danger.

Whatever he was enduring, the redhead kept his pain to himself, and he held to his post even as his commander did. He knew the role Sogan's faster response had left to him, and he was too much a Commando to do other than carry it. Anything less would neither serve their primary assignment nor, in all probability, do their companions any good.

Suddenly Bandit swept up over the lip of the falls. She made straight for Islaen. *Varn and Bethe swimming! Safe soon!*

The woman's head snapped up. "You're sure?"

Bandit watched! Couldn't help! Couldn't bother Varn! Couldn't talk while Islaen and Jake were working!

"You did right, love. Thank you. Watch them again and bring us any further news, but don't interfere if it would cause trouble."

Bandit will be careful!

The guerrilla sighed in her heart. If only she could join her senses directly with the Jadite the way Sogan did . . .

Karmikel watched the excited gurry plummet out of sight again. "Islaen!" he roared. "In the name of space, what did she say? Are they . . ."

"Sorry, Jake. They're fine, apparently."

The off-world craft fairly leaped as a new eddy struck her, nearly pulling the rope out of the Colonel's hands despite the tightness of her hold.

For the next several minutes the two guerrillas fought to maintain their control over the bucking vessel. They had to hold her now, with the falls only yards, feet, away.

They were on the edge! "Inside!" the Colonel ordered even as she vaulted over the side. A few seconds later a soft, squelching thud announced that her companion had succeeded in obeying.

Both grabbed their paddles. This was the actual moment of descent and the most dangerous part of the whole endeavor. They were moving frighteningly fast over the roughest stretch they had yet encountered, and at the end of it gaped the trench created by the pounding of the river. They would have to skim out into the quieter area some distance from the falls and not allow themselves to be caught and driven under by the fury directly below.

The Commandos were well trained in the handling of all manner of watercraft, and they managed this one well, but still, each of them wished for the Arcturian's skilled help as they began that wild descent. Even more strongly, they wished themselves out of this entirely.

The Amazoonan boat accepted their guidance as she hurtled down the rough slide, and she responded at the end as they willed. She hit bottom, not directly, but at an angle that carried her outward, away from the deadly danger of the falls. Spurred by her passengers' frantic paddling, she shot away from the drop, into the pool it had formed and then into the normally flowing river beyond.

As soon as they found themselves well clear, the off-worlders eased their efforts and returned to their previous cruising speed.

At that point, they had time to think. They had made it down safely, but what of the others? They began to search the water and land around them for some sign of their comrades.

Islaen's questing mind met her consort's, and in another moment she had spotted the missing guerrillas sitting huddled together among the vegetation on the left-hand bank not very far from them.

In a matter of minutes she and Jake Karmikel had brought the boat in and made her fast to two strong young trees.

The Commando-Colonel's eyes bored almost hungrily into the pair awaiting them on the shore. The two remained perfectly still as sensitive, skilled fingers seemed to probe every cell in their bodies.

In the end, Islaen withdrew. They were sound, or sound enough. Both were soaked through, of course, and obviously spent after their struggle against the Maiden. Bethe was definitely the worse off of the two, as was only to be expected. She sat hunched up, as if all the life had been leeched from her, and her face was white and strained, although she managed a real smile in greeting to them.

Sogan felt more than a little shaky himself, but by seemingly casually using the tree nearest him for support, he was able to get to his feet reasonably smoothly. He told the spacer to stay where she was, then slid down the short height of the bank into the boat.

Karmikel steadied him until he found his balance, assistance he normally would scarcely have required but for which he was grateful now.

Jake's fingers remained tight on his arm. "Sogan . . ." he began.

The Arcturian shook his head. "She needs you. Take care of her. I will help Islaen finish up here."

The other man nodded and left him quickly without speaking again.

Varn joined the auburn-haired woman. When he faced the bank again, the redhead had already folded Bethe in his arms. He smiled. *That will benefit her more right now than any fire or formal treatment could.*

You're a good man, Varn Tarl Sogan, Islaen Connor told him softly. She eyed him. *You could do with a bit of comforting yourself.*

He smiled again. *I am all right, just somewhat spent. I swallowed a lot less water.*

I wish neither of you had swallowed any of it, she replied with feeling, then shrugged and willed the last wisps of fear out of her mind. *You were both lucky. There wouldn't have been any spring leeches around the falls, and the Maiden runs pretty clean. I've confirmed that you didn't pick up lesser parasites or toxin-forming organisms, and we can trust our shots to stop anything else. Even if some bug does slip by them, you shouldn't begin showing symptoms until well after this is all over.*

If that is what you mean by "comfort," Colonel Connor . . .

She smiled. *Hardly, Admiral. It was just an observation.*

What is our next move? he inquired more seriously.

Make camp. You two're done, and Jake and I aren't in much better shape. We'll get started now if you feel up to it. Otherwise, I'll wait a few more minutes and roust out Jake. Bethe really isn't able for additional duties tonight.

Leave them be. I can manage, as you well know, or you would not have made the suggestion. —Let us finish with the boat first and then see about some dinner. The rest will hold until after that.

Islaen watched Varn slip yet another large piece of his ration cake to the seemingly ever-hungry gurry. *You know,* she observed casually as she shifted into a more comfortable position, *I used to do precisely the same thing with our family pets when I didn't like my dinner. I was only about five at the time, of course.*

Bandit's not a pet! the Jadite protested hotly. *Bethe just says that!*

"I know, love. I was only making a comparison." She smiled at her husband as she spoke. They were sitting far enough apart from the other couple that she could tease him a little without embarrassing him too greatly even should they become aware of what was going on. They would not be able to hear enough of what she was actually saying to the gurry to guess the rest.

In point of fact, Varn had been doing precisely what she had stated. Amazoonans were mad for the taste of fish, the stronger the better, and used a powerful emulsion comprised of it in or with nearly everything they ate including the foodstuffs they prepared for use in survival situations. Sogan, on the other hand, had always detested most seafoods.

The Arcturian scowled. *She likes this stuff.* There was some surprise in that. Like humans, gurries were omnivorous, but they much preferred vegetable food, resorting to flesh only in times of real need.

Food good! the hen informed him. *Not fish! Only tastes like it!*

"Aye, but Varn hates that, as we all well know." The woman eyed him. *There's no point in inflicting punishment on yourself. Next time, grab one of our own packets. The rest of us don't mind these.*

The former Admiral stiffened. *Amazoonan supplies do me no harm, and they are more perishable than Federation rations. We will need everything we have if we must walk out after our attack.*

I dislike martyrs, Admiral, she said but gave it up. She supposed she would not receive the suggestion that she accept special treatment very kindly, either. "Come on, Bandit. You've certainly had more than enough. It's time to set up the hammocks, and I want you to help me."

Bandit will help! How?

"Fly up to the canopy and make sure we don't inadvertently pick any ant trees for our supports."

All trees here have ants!

"These are special." Using mental images to reinforce her words, the Commando described what signs to seek in the crown to identify a tree that was likely to be involved in such a relationship. They did not need an attack by a horde of furious biting insects to top off the efforts and troubles of the day. "While you're up there, check for dead branches. Such things do fall occasionally, and I'd prefer that it not be on top of one of us."

Yes, Islaen!

Wait a minute, Colonel, Sogan said. *I will give you a hand with the hammocks.*

He hastily swallowed the remainder of his portion, grimacing involuntarily at the powerful taste.

He realized he was to a certain extent playing the fool with his stubbornness and gave a rueful shake of his head. *I like these Amazoonans, Islaen Connor, but I am right glad that we are not required to live among them for any length of time.*

Jake kept his arm around Bethe Danlo, wanting and needing the contact with her as much as he knew she needed him. Neither spoke while they ate. Few of those accustomed to life in space delayed a meal with talk, never knowing when an emergency would arise to interrupt or terminate it.

He watched the woman carefully, however, trying to detect any sign of injury on her that the Colonel's talent might have missed.

There was no indication of anything amiss in the way she ate. Bethe devoured her packet without any urging. In truth, she would have welcomed a second helping despite its strong fishy flavor, but she said nothing about that. Varn Tarl Sogan was not the only one who was aware that they would all have to tighten their belts if by some ill chance they could not arrange for an airlift home after their job was done.

She felt her husband's eyes on her and looked up at him with a mischievous smile. "Aye, Comrade?"

"I'm just relieved to see you eating well," he said, embarrassed that she had caught him.

"A stiff swim is supposed to build the appetite." She shuddered then. "I've never felt so helpless, Jake, so powerless to do anything whatsoever for myself. I was certain I was going to die."

"I wasn't too happy myself," he told her, "and not being able to come to you made it all a galaxy worse."

"Varn was just nearer . . ."

"Nearer, hell! I've never seen a man move that fast. He was in the boat before I rightly realized you were in trouble."

"That was because of his link with Islaen."

"Aye. I suppose so. —I'm glad he lifted before I did. I have to be. Space! I knew our Admiral was damn good in the water, but I hadn't realized he'd become half a fish."

She smiled. "Lucky for me that he is."

"Lucky for us both," the Noreenan corrected gently. "I owe him for this one."

His eyes went to their companions as he spoke. Suddenly he laughed softly. "Look at those two fussing over Bandit," he whispered.

"Laugh on the other side of your face, friend. She manages both of us very nicely, and she can't even talk directly to us."

"I know, but it is funny watching someone else at it." Especially the normally self-conscious former Admiral.

The redhead yawned. "How about knocking out? Since our comrades kindly put up the hammocks, I'm minded to make use of them."

"And to get into dry clothes," Bethe agreed fervently. "I'm looking forward to that more than anything else right now." Almost painfully so. She was infinitely glad they had decided to keep this set on the previous evening and hold the spares for tonight. It was a luxury they would not enjoy again until this already cursed mission was behind them.

"Enjoy them while you've got them," Karmikel replied gloomily. "It'll probably be pouring soon, and we'll be soaked again as soon as we have to roll out for our watches."

"We drew the last slots, at least, so we'll have a nice long nap under the tarp first." She yawned. "By all the old gods, I'm dead spent! —Come on, Comrade. Let's not waste any more of our off time sitting here."

Their sleeping arrangements were reasonably comfortable. Jake's hammock and Bethe's were hung so closely together that they almost touched, as were Islaen's and Varn's, although the

four were fixed to their own trees. One of the tarps had been
fastened over each pair to ward off the inevitable rain. The
sturdy slings, designed as they were for Amazoonan proportions, were more than adequately large enough for the off-
worlders and allowed for the maximum possible circulation of
air. Islaen Connor had already distributed their packs and the
essential gnat nets, putting them on the hammocks where they
would remain dry and free of ground-dwelling pests.

Karmikel started pulling his tunic open even before he got to
his assigned place, but he stopped short when he reached for
his pack.

"Sogan, are you two trying to be funny?" he demanded in
obviously foul humor.

His companions joined him.

"What's wrong?" demanded the Commando-Colonel. "It's
well fastened, and that is definitely your pack."

"I thought you were supposed to be watching out for ant
trees," he said, pointing to what looked like a solid carpet of
tiny red insects busily moving in two well-ordered columns
along the whole of the hammock and its contents.

Islaen bent to get a closer look at the creatures. "They're leaf
cutters, not real tree ants," she declared after a moment.

"I can see that myself, Colonel," he replied sarcastically.
"They are, however, very proper ants of some sort, as this
world defines them, and they're occupying my bed."

Bandit did wrong? the gurry wailed. *Bandit tried to
find . . .*

"No, love. You did fine. We didn't tell you to look for
these."

"No matter," Jake said gruffly, ashamed for having upset the
little Jadite. He should have known anyway that his comrades
would not have indulged in that sort of sport, especially not
after all they had endured in these last several days. "I'll just
shake them off and find myself another pole. —Unless you
could talk the miseries into leaving of their own accord and
then stay away, Admiral."

Varn smiled and closed his eyes dramatically, in keeping
with the other's restored humor.

It was difficult for him to think visually rather than in words,
but he concentrated on sending the images, concepts, he
wanted to the minute host. The insects were not angry or

troubled. They had merely discovered the hammock and were using it as a convenient bridge between the tree nearest their nest, which was probably underground, and the one whose leaves they were currently harvesting. At least, those heading in one direction were unburdened while their fellows in the returning column all bore pieces of leaves and other greenery. He worked to transmit the picture of the disruption the orderly troop would suffer when Jake Karmikel shook out the hammock, scattering the foragers in every directions, and to instill the idea of returning to their normal overland route.

It was but an exercise, of course. Sogan had never had much success in influencing horde insects, not in numbers like this.

Bethe's gasp caused his eyes to open. He almost stopped transmitting in his amazement. The ants were retreating. The whole host was calmly and purposefully returning to the trunk from which they had been issuing and were moving from there to the ground.

The Noreenan man looked from the departing insects to his comrade. "I was just joking, Admiral," he said in something like awe.

"So was I, friend."

Varn did it! Bandit cooed with as much pride as if she had accomplished the feat herself.

"That he did, love," the Colonel agreed. "Varn, while you're at it . . ." She made a sweeping motion with her arm both to indicate and to discourage the cloud of flying things that were their perpetual escorts.

The Arcturian's eyes slitted, but he shook his head after a few moments. "No luck this time. Their intelligence level is much lower, and they are hungry for their prey. I could discourage a few of them, but not this multitude."

"Never mind. It was just worth the try." She looked at him thoughtfully. "First the snake, then the spring leech, and now these ants. Your talents seems to be particularly effective with Amazoon's creatures. That may prove useful to us before we see the end of all this. —You have the first watch, Admiral. As for the rest of us, I suggest that we knock out now. I'll guarantee that tomorrow's not going to be any shorter and probably no easier than today was."

THIRTEEN

THE WAR PRINCE sighed as he rolled up the clothes he had worn the previous day and stuffed them into his pack. They were scarcely any drier than they had been when he had hung them on the rope stretched above his hammock for that purpose.

He had not changed until after his watch, so the rain, which had begun without preamble during the latter part of it, had not gotten to the fresh set. The respite had been all too temporary. Amazoon's heat and humidity had rapidly done their work, and already everything was damp enough to be uncomfortable, before he had even begun to move about in any real sense. The only purpose in changing from now on would be to air the garments and prevent the inevitable rot of the jungle from taking hold too rapidly, that and to cleanse his own skin. The corrugated mass of scar tissue covering his back was particularly vulnerable to infection by many of the organisms flourishing in this wretched climate.

As he worked to dismantle his hammock, his mind almost automatically ranged the jungle around them. He picked up no surprising readings. Everything was about the same as it had been yesterday and probably every yesterday for millennia. Change did not occur often or with any great speed in a stable and ultralush environment such as this.

The Arcturian started when he turned his attention to their vessel, and he called out in warning to Karmikel, who had been about to board her.

The Noreenan turned. "What's wrong, Admiral? More ants?"

"Not quite, but we do have a passenger."

He had no difficulty in contacting and influencing this creature, and in the space of a couple of breaths, a long, thick-bodied reptile began slithering over the side, back into the water from whence it had come.

Jake gave a silent whistle. "Son of a Scythian ape! That snake's got to be thirty feet long!"

"A water snake. It meant no harm, but they are venomous. Remember, we were warned about their penchant for napping on floating debris?"

"Guerrillas who forget things like that don't live too long, my friend.—Any other wildlife aboard?"

"Nothing for us to worry about. The snake would have discouraged most other potential visitors."

"It discourages me," he remarked dryly. "This is already shaping up into another wonderful day, and I have a nasty feeling it'll probably surpass its beginning."

The redhead's forebodings proved well founded, at least insofar as the labor required of the off-worlders was concerned. They had been on the water less than an hour when the nature of the Maiden began to change very perceptibly. They had entered the true lowlands at last. There was little fall to spur the river's flow, and in place of the fast, rapid-infested stream of the previous day, it now ran slowly over a broader course that was in actuality a confusion of multiple channels sometimes linked, sometimes separated by an ever-increasing number of gravel and mud banks. With the loss of its speed, it could no longer support so heavy a load of silt and other debris. The light things, the branches and greenery, still floated with it, but the stones and gravel and soil precipitated out, silting the bottom and accumulating to such a degree in places that the bed was filled, and the water was compelled to cut yet another channel for itself.

Constant vigilance and quick action were needed to keep them from grounding on a mud bank or ripping the hull open on some obstacle projecting from an entirely too close bottom. Most of the work had to be done with the poles, a slow, killing pulling and pushing that left every muscle taxed and strained.

Islaen Connor set her jaw tightly, determined to let no sign of her weariness escape her. The others were no less tired, no

less drained by the endless heat. While they held up, she was
not about to give over.

She had no right to do so. She commanded the unit, and hers
had been the decision to go on with the mission.

Grimly the Commando-Colonel drove her pole into the
riverbed. This part of it would end eventually, she thought,
when the Maiden joined the Matron. If it did not finish her
first . . .

A shock of pure, agonizing energy ran up the metal rod. She
screamed in surprise and pain, then screamed again as a
second, even stronger charge ripped into her.

She tried to drop the pole, but her hands were frozen to it,
fastened firmly by the power of the current racing through it.
A third jolt . . .

Something heavy and dark struck her arms. There was a
sickening crack and simultaneous stab of intense pain, then a
welcome blackness engulfed her.

The woman moaned and struggled to sit up only to find
herself restrained by gentle, vise-strong hands.

"Easy," Varn cautioned. "Let the renewer finish its work."

She settled back in his arms. "Do your worst," she said in a
voice that she could not quite force to assume its normal
strength.

Bethe was the one who was handling the ray. She continued
to direct it onto the Noreenan's forearm for a few seconds
longer before finally nodding her satisfaction and switching it
off. "Overhaul complete, Colonel. You should be as good as
new now."

Islaen flexed her arm. "No pain there. Thanks." She looked
at the four anxious faces around her. "Who's minding the
boat?"

"She's tied," Jake told her curtly, dismissing that question.
"How do you feel?"

"Fine. A bit tired. —What happened, anyway?"

"Your pole apparently tipped a chargefish, a big one," her
husband informed her.

Her brows lifted. "That'd explain the shocks, right enough."
It also explained the fear she was picking up from her friends.
The Spirit ruling space and Amazoon's Green Lady had both
been guarding her. Had her heartbeat been out of sync, even

slightly out of sync, with the pulse of the fish's current, she would almost certainly have been killed. As it was, she might have suffered severe damage.

It was more difficult to turn her mind inward than to examine another, but she bent her will to it and ran a thorough check on herself.

The woman smiled at last. "I'm sound out, Comrades. No ill effects at all."

Islaen's not sick? Bandit pressed.

"No, love. As soon as I catch my wind a bit, I'll be ready to go back to work."

"When space turns white, you will!" snapped the Arcturian.

Islaen laughed. "We'll see, Admiral." Her large eyes flickered to the renewer. "Now I know one part of it. What about that?"

"We had to break the current's grip," Sogan explained. "I used my pack to do it, but the blow snapped your arm."

"That's no way to treat your commanding officer, Admiral," she told him severely.

The Colonel squirmed in his hold. When he would not release her, she gave it up and allowed him to raise her to a more upright position. His strength and the tenderness of his touch both felt good to her just then, and she was not really minded to battle against them.

"My pole is long gone, I suppose?"

"Not at all," Karmikel replied. "I fished it out." He scowled. "What in space or beyond it moved those Amazoonans to make it out of metal, I'll never know."

"Probably the fact that anything else would rot too quickly. I will mention that they might consider using something that isn't quite so good a conductor, though. Assuming anyone'll believe me." Islaen shook her head. "I must've set that bloody stick right down on its back. I couldn't have managed it if I were trying." Her expression clouded. "I hope I didn't hurt the poor thing very badly."

"Space!" Varn exploded, then added a comment under his breath in his own language.

The Jadite chirped in surprise. *But, Varn, fish only scared! Protecting itself!*

He did not even try to answer her. There was no point in arguing with either of these two on this sort of subject.

Besides, their comrades were already laughing at him. It was more a release of tension than anything else, but he still did not care to fuel their merriment any further.

He settled Islaen against the side. "Since we have decided the good Colonel is going to survive, I suggest we continue with our voyage. The sooner we reach the Matron, the sooner we shall get some ease. We are not likely to find any before then."

FOURTEEN

ISLAEN LEANED ON her pole. It had been a struggle to convince her companions to allow her to resume her full share of the team's work. She had won in the end, but it was not an enjoyable victory.

She looked from one to the other of her comrades and found them all gray with weariness.

That settled it in her mind. They would not reach the Matron before nightfall no matter what they did, and she knew there was a rough and very tricky stretch to be negotiated before the two rivers joined. They were not fit to face that now, and if they kept on any farther, they would be worth little in any emergency that might arise. She gave the order to put ashore at once and prepare their evening's camp.

More to give them all a brief rest before they had to start slashing away at the tangle than from any real hunger, she suggested that they eat immediately, a proposal the others were quick to second.

Bandit perched expectantly on Varn's knee, knowing she would get the largest portion from him. She purred and then gave several impatient whistles when the anticipated meal was slow in coming.

"Wait a minute, will you," the Colonel, whose turn it was to cook, chided. "Even rations take a little while to heat up."

When they were ready, she distributed the sizzling packets and sat down opposite her husband. He had opened his share and was already breaking off a big chunk for the eager gurry. *That's your dinner. Don't give all of it to Her.*

The Jadite protested with a squawk muffled by the food filling her bill. *Bandit can't eat Varn's share! Too much!*

The Arcturian frowned. *Power down, Islaen. What I do with this is my business.*

Her chin lifted at that. *True enough, but your weight's still down after some of the legitimate wounds you've taken. You're blowing up with the ship needlessly on this one, playing the long-suffering soldier when perfectly edible food is available, and I don't want to find that you've dropped another ten pounds as a result.*

There is small chance of that. I am not a fool.

The woman finished her portion quickly without speaking again. She brushed the last crumbs off her hands and looked around. Jake Karmikel was finished as well.

"Let's take a walk, Jake. The tangle's at its worst at the water's edge. If we go in a bit, we might find a spot where we can hang the hammocks without having to do quite so much hacking first."

"Sure thing, Colonel."

"What about us?" Bethe asked her.

"Finish eating and start pulling our camp gear together. We won't be long. If we can't find anything suitable right off, we'll come back." She glanced at her consort. "Any welcoming committees we should know about?"

He listened for several moments before shaking his head. "No. Just the usual fauna. Those who will view us as prey will merely replace the ones buzzing around our heads now."

The former Admiral answered smoothly, but he lowered his head as soon as the pair disappeared behind the screening vegetation.

What else could he have expected, he thought glumly. After that incident with the spring leech, the Commando-Colonel would have to be stark mad to ask him to accompany her into any wilderness while she had more competent help available to her.

Varn's busy! Feeding Bandit!

"Truly." He smiled despite himself and caressed the soft brown feathers with the tips of his fingers. It had been a happy and lucky day when Islaen Connor and he had planeted on Jade of Kuan Yin.

* * *

The two Noreenans had pushed their way only a few feet from the camp before they were completely out of sight and also out of hearing of it.

"We're riding a comet's tail, Colonel," the Captain remarked. "There's no inner country here, just a series of miserable little overgrown mud banks set between various segments of the river."

Islaen sighed. "That's why I said we'd be back right away. It is worth the look, though, just in case. We're all about done, and anything that'd save us a bit of work would be a blessing." She was also very irritated with Varn Tarl Sogan and wanted to get out of his company for a while before she reamed him for a fact, but of that, she would not speak to this man or to any other.

The end of their quest came quickly. Karmikel slashed a wall of vines apart only to see a channel of the fragmented river glistening a few feet away.

He had expected nothing else, but still, he swung at the vegetation again in disgust.

"Jake, watch out!"

Too late, he saw the dirty white semicircular mass of what appeared to be some sort of crude paper clinging to the lower branches of a young sapling. He could not stop the fall of his hatchet, nor could he turn it completely enough. It missed the thing's center but sliced cleanly through its outer edge.

He had not pulled the axe free again before the air was filled with a fierce buzzing and both humans were literally covered by a swarm of inch-long, bright yellow insects armed with stingers that seemed to extend the length of the creatures' bodies.

Shoving the woman before him, the Commando-Captain raced for the riverbank. He pushed Islaen into the murky water and leaped in after her.

That cleared the crown wasps off their bodies, but it did not stop the assault. The maddened swarm stayed with them, hovering only inches above the water, waiting.

The Colonel stripped off her tunic and pulled it over her head, so arranging it that only her nose and mouth were exposed. The redhead followed suit.

Breathing was a horror. As soon as they broke water, the

insects dove. The tough material protected most of their faces, but there was no defense for nostrils and lips. Even their mouths and upper throats were not spared, for they could not bite all of the wasps forcing their way in between their lips and teeth, and many struck there as well, some of them more than once. Unlike their counterparts on a number of other planets, these did not lose their stingers after a single use, although their store of venom was much reduced following a strike and was temporarily totally depleted after the second.

Both endured their persecution long enough to draw a deep breath before seeking refuge under the surface again.

The Commando-Colonel's mind reached out. She could sense Varn's seeking hers. He had felt the pain and terror of the attack—she had raised no shields during these last, confused seconds—and the wasps' fury, but this was no mere human assault, and he was too battle-trained to come charging after them without at least some idea of what had happened and what he might expect to face. She described as well as she was able the accident and its aftermath and tried to venture a guess as to their present situation.

Her lungs were screaming for air before she finished, and she was forced to break off, this time taking care to screen her transmissions very well, and go to the surface once more.

The wasps' attack was worse, perceptibly worse, than she had endured on her previous rise. There seemed to be no end to the vicious insects or to their hatred of the human intruders. *Varn, can you help us at all?*

I can try, he responded grimly.

Immediately she became aware of the power flowing out from the Arcturian. It held for nearly a minute, then ceased altogether. Despair replaced it. *They are in a total frenzy. I cannot move them.*

Determination firmed within him. *A blaster set at broad beam . . .*

With us half an inch under the surface? We'll wait it out, thank you.

She had to breathe. When she was again able to resume contact, Islaen found his will set as a stubborn wall against her. *I know enough to aim high, Islaen Connor. As for waiting, think again. It is not one swarm that you are facing but many, and more are arriving every few seconds. Apparently, an*

attack against one nest is viewed as an attack against every-
thing in the vicinity on Amazoon of Indra.

Are your circuits blown? You can't fight numbers like that.

I must, and now. There will be too many soon . . .

There are too many now! Stay put.

How long can you two survive the way you are?

However long we have to survive, she snapped. *Even if we
don't, it's better that two of us should go than all of us.*

The anger sapped the air from her lungs. She had to rise yet
again. When she returned, she was shaken, but the Commando
made herself reestablish contact immediately.

It was to find Varn Tarl Sogan already on the move. Her
hands coiled into tight fists. *Return to the boat, Captain. That
is an order. You, Bethe, and Bandit are to remain there until
this is over and it's safe for you to proceed.*

She could feel his rage—and his anguish—but she was his
commander, and she had left him without choice. He obeyed.

Tears momentarily cleared the muddy water from the woman's eyes. She was scared and sick and hurt, and she did not
want to die like this.

A hand sought and found hers. Jake, too, was nearly
overwhelmed with helplessness and fear. In his misery, he tried
to comfort her and to take comfort from her . . .

Suddenly the Captain stiffened. He tugged at her hand to
make her follow him. Islaen could see no purpose to moving,
knowing the ever-growing swarm would only come after them,
but she went with him.

The off-worlders traveled downriver about thirty yards until
the stream curved, cutting sharply into the bank. She understood then and dove for the hollow even as Karmikel started to
push her into it.

Both drew a desperately needed breath. They were not
secure, not by any means, but the overhang provided some
protection, made it difficult for the wasps to come at them and
drastically cut down on the numbers of those able to do so at
any given time. At least, they now had a chance, a better
chance, of surviving this siege.

His defeat left the war prince with only one already-failed
weapon with which to fight for his comrades' lives, for his
consort's life. It was all he had, and so he concentrated on

wielding it, on trying to calm and dismiss the enraged horde battering the friends he was otherwise powerless to aid.

He poured more and more of his energy into his effort until Islaen Connor, who could feel the force of his sending, feared that he might draw upon the strength sustaining his very life as he had done in the space above Jade of Kuan Yin.

Another mind stream joined the former Admiral's. Bandit had entered the fight, reinforcing Varn's massive effort and adding her own special brand of peace and goodwill. In another moment the Colonel had linked with them as well.

It was but poor help that she was able to provide. She was weakened by her ordeal and more so by the need to surface every few minutes for air and endure the punishment waiting for her there, but what she could do to aid their cause, she must. Sogan needed whatever support she could give him.

She strove to transfuse her strength into him, to replenish the energy he was pouring out of himself, rather than to directly influence the insect host. The mental reserves, the body, upon which the Arcturian's will had to draw were all too finite. He had almost died on Jade . . .

The crown wasps were responding!

They did not all do so in the same moment, nor did they withdraw at once, but the fury, of which she was fully sensible as a result of her link with Varn, gradually went out of them until it was entirely gone.

For the first time nothing molested Jake or her when they broke the surface to breathe, and the little strip of sky visible from their refuge was free of yellow, sting-tipped fliers.

"Wait," the woman cautioned her comrade in a scarcely audible whisper. "Let's be sure." —*Varn, tell us when we can move.*

Soon. They have returned to their own places, but some of those are near. We cannot chance rousing them afresh.

Minutes passed. Five. Ten. At last the war prince called to her again. *Come ahead. Follow the bank until the overhang ends, then go ashore. We shall meet you there.*

FIFTEEN

VARN TARL SOGAN had to fight himself not to race madly, mindlessly, to the place where he would join his consort. He compelled himself to prepare the first-aid kits that he and Bethe must carry and then to move carefully through the choking vegetation. Act thoughtlessly now, and they could wind up in as much trouble as that which their comrades had so narrowly escaped.

Or were trying to escape. They had not seen Islaen or Jake yet.

By using his contact with the Colonel to guide him, the dark-eyed Commando reached the place where the pair were to emerge just as they rose up out of the water.

His eyes closed momentarily at the sight of them. They were wet, of course, and incredibly muddy, but their faces . . . People had died from such damage. All the area around the nose and lips was blackened and grotesquely swollen, and there had been strikes to other parts of the head as well, plenty of them, probably taken during their dash to reach the river.

Both staggered and stumbled when they tried to take their weight from the Maiden's support. He leaped forward, first lifting the Colonel to the bank and then guiding and supporting Karmikel until he could ease him to the ground.

"Bethe, he is yours," Sogan said as he reached for the medical kit he had brought. He would care for Islaen Connor himself.

Ripping her tunic open, he quickly injected her with antivenin to counter the wasps' poison and with antihistamine to combat the swelling. Antibiotics followed. In this accursed

99

jungle, any untreated wound was going to become badly
infected in very short order, and there was greater danger of
that from these minute punctures than there would have been
from a large, freely bleeding gash. One other vial, he kept
ready but did not believe he would have to use, not now. If
anaphylactic shock were going to set in, she and Jake would
have been dead long since.

He washed her face next, using clean water from his
canteen. Varn worked carefully and very gently, for her bruised
flesh was tender, but he was thorough. Antibiotics or none, no
foreign matter could be allowed to remain sealed under the
layer of soothing, protective ointment he was going to apply.

The renewer, too, he used. It helped, but there was only so
much even that could do in this case. A great part of the swelling
disfiguring the Noreenan's face was the work of the wasps'
venom, and it would take the slower-acting shots to bring it down.

After that, there was no more immediate aid that he could
give her.

The Arcturian looked over his shoulder. Bethe was finished
with her patient as well. She came to her feet when she saw that
he was ready and walked as far as the riverbank. He joined her
there.

"How is he?"

"Nothing seriously amiss, praise the Spirit of Space.
—Islaen?"

"The same."

"Those two aren't going anywhere for a while under their
own jets, Varn."

"I know. You stay with them. I will bring the boat. We can
camp here." Fortunately, they had not yet unloaded any of the
gear. "That will be easier than trying to carry them back
through this tangle. —Bandit, remain behind as well. If Islaen
or Jake start turning sour, I want to know it right away."

Yes, Varn!

"Do you think that's likely to happen?" the demolitions
expert asked with fresh concern.

"No. I will just feel better for keeping in direct contact. At
any rate, I shall not be long."

Varn settled Islaen in her hammock and gently spread her
spider silk blanket over her to combat the chill of the

poison-induced fever. He stood looking down at her, at a loss
for something more to do for her yet unwilling to leave her so
soon.

She managed to curve her sore lips into a smile. *Sit beside
me awhile. The hammock's more than big enough, and I'm not
the kind of hurt that you'd have to be afraid of jostling me.*

He obeyed. *How are you feeling now?*

Would you believe me if I said fine?

No.

Pure rotten, then. She tossed her head restlessly. *It'll pass
off soon enough, I suppose.*

His hand brushed her forehead and then closed over hers.
You are so hot.

*That's hardly surprising, considering. I'll just have to try to
sleep it off and wait for the antivenin to complete its job.* She
sighed. *A pity it's not really specific for wasp stings. I'd be
over it by now if it were.*

Sogan's head lowered. *I tried to drive them off,* he whispered. *I could do nothing while they were in that frenzy . . .*

Varn, stop it! Islaen told him sharply. *You chased them as
soon as you could, and you kept the spring leeches away from
us, didn't you? That mud bank must've been alive with the little
monsters.*

It was, he admitted. *You were both lucky none had already
attached themselves.*

*Then stop flogging yourself because there are limits to what
your talent can do. We're all a galaxy better off because of it.*
Her eyes closed. *Besides, I'm simply too tired right now to be
arguing with you.*

Sorry, my Islaen, the former Admiral said, instantly contrite.

She smiled but seized on the opportunity to turn the subject
entirely. *How are you going to manage the watch?*

*The three of us will do fine. We have divided up the night
evenly, with Bandit taking the last slot.*

She did not think to question that. The gurry was neither a
cute pet nor a child despite her winning ways and love of
comfort. She was an adult member of an intelligent, highly
successful species and was fully capable of assuming her share
of responsibility for their safety. She had proven that time and
time again since she had joined her life with theirs.

It was at Sogan that the Commando-Colonel looked with

some doubt. *You have to be exhausted,* she said quietly. *Why don't you knock out now and take the final turn yourself?*

He shook his head. *I will crash once I do lie down. I am better off keeping going and getting my stint over as quickly as possible.*

He turned at the Jadite's approach. "How is our other patient?"

Jake's asleep now! she answered.

"Good." He came to his feet. "Islaen should sleep, too, and you as well, small one. You must be ready for your work later on."

Bandit will stay with Islaen! As she spoke, she snuggled down beside the woman.

Varn bent over and kissed his consort tenderly on the forehead. *Rest well, my Islaen.*

The Noreenan's mind touched his in a soft caress, then she let him go.

A warmth remained inside her, but there was a shadow with it that deepened as she turned her conscious thoughts upon it. No one appreciated better than Islaen Connor how easily this wonder could be riven from her. What would she do then, she wondered. What she shared with Varn Tarl Sogan was a brightness and a bulwark amid the violence that ruled so much of her life.

Her eyes closed. How she needed him! Sometimes she thought that his love was the only thing that kept her mind and spirit from shattering under the pressure and danger of her work.

Her work. War was her business, she thought wearily. It always would be now. The whole of her adult life had been devoted to combat of one sort or another, ever since she was a recruit so young that her parents had to sign her enlistment forms. At that time, there had been no hint of an end to the decades-old War between the Federation and the Arcturian Empire, but at least that conclusion had been a goal for which one could strive. She had known much of horror in the years that followed her stint in Basic training. She had brought death and had seen close friends die and had watched still others, strangers but still comrades, fall in the cause for which they all were fighting, but always, there had been the glimmering hope, ever strengthening as the tide inexorably turned against the Empire, of an eventual time of peace and normalcy.

For most of her ultrasystem's soldiers that had indeed more or less come to pass, but it was several years now since the treaty closing the great War had been signed, and there had been no return to Noreen's pastures for her. Another, in its way even more vicious war had claimed her services, hers and Jake's and Bethe's and even Varn's. Throughout the Federation, renegades, human vermin, strove to take advantage of the confusion still reigning in many Sectors to carve fortunes and even petty domains for themselves, threatening to annihilate from within everything countless men and women had suffered and died to preserve. Duty was too much a part of her life for her to walk away from this second challenge, although she realized full well that it would never be ended, not in the course of her lifetime.

Varn Tarl Sogan was, if anything, even more powerfully moved by the same considerations. If the Navy and the sense of responsibility it fostered had become her life, he had quite literally been bred to that ethic. He was a war prince in truth, although the prerogatives of that rank were no longer his to enjoy, a man highly born, of the Emperor's own line, in the warrior caste of an intensely military society. As such, he had learned to put himself behind what he held to be his duty, and as an officer of the highest rank, he had learned to think and judge for himself in need as well as to blindly obey. That combination had worked to his great hurt in the end.

His sense of honor—the Empire's as well as personal—an innate justice, and his basic humanity and compassion had forced him to do the unthinkable, to refuse to follow the order of the superior whose insanity none had then recognized and thus spare Thorne of Brandine from a total burn-off.

That mercy had received none in return. His people, in the pain of their defeat, had needed a scapegoat, one against whom they could vent their outrage and hate. He had lost his Admiral's rank and his place in his own caste. His children had been slaughtered to eradicate his seed from the race, and his consort and concubines had embraced their daggers in their shame. He himself had been flogged through his own fleet and his supposedly lifeless body cast adrift in space in an ancient lifecraft, which then crossed the better part of the galaxy and very nearly passed out of it. Only raw luck had brought him near enough to be rescued by the Doritan mining settlement, where he had been taken for a victim of the Arcturians rather than one of that much-hated race himself.

The sale of the lifecraft had allowed him to purchase the then-derelict *Fairest Maid*, and for the next three years, he had roamed the rim, maintaining himself and his freighter in an existence without hope or purpose. Only pure stubbornness and an anger against both his people and their cruel gods had prevented him from taking the course reason would have dictated as inevitable for one of his caste in such circumstances.

His chance meeting with her unit on Visnu of Brahmin had changed all that. His performance there had gained for him entry first into the Navy and then the Commandos, giving him purpose and real work once more, although he would never again be able to hold higher rank than he now did or be granted a command befitting his training and experience. It was too necessary to conceal his true history, even if one of his race would ever be entrusted with such a position in the Navy he had once battled so fiercely.

That was stark injustice. In the short time since he had joined with her company, Sogan had so conducted himself in defense of the planets and peoples of his former enemies that he had become the Federation's most highly decorated soldier with seven class-one heroism citations to his credit, one more than she herself had earned.

Islaen sighed in her heart. Varn was a man who fought well, not one who loved violence for its own sake. Like herself, he accepted the stark necessity of what they did and recognized full well that the populations of cities, that entire colonies, now lived directly as a result of their activities, but he, too, longed occasionally for peace—and probably more frequently and deeply than he permitted her to realize—or for a greater share of peace than they were ever likely to have.

She tossed her head in despair. She could not give him that, no more than she could arrange for him to have the rank he merited or the kind of command he was meant to hold. Perhaps she had no right even to allow him to love her, knowing how much of himself he had invested in her, how devastating her loss would be for him who had already seen all he had once

valued in his life shattered. There was just too much danger in
their profession . . .

Bandit stirred beside her. *Islaen?*

She started. "Sorry, love."

The guerrilla made herself relax. This would accomplish
nothing except weary her further and drain away reserves she
needed for healing her actual injuries. Steeling herself, she
forced the dark mood from her mind and willed herself to
sleep.

The war prince continued to conceal the heaviness weighing
his spirit as he took his position. It was understandable enough,
he supposed. He had well nigh driven himself into a collapse
in his efforts to banish the wasps, and some sort of reaction was
only to be expected, especially with everything else they had
endured of late—the killing physical labor, the unremitting
heat, their losses and near losses.

He shook his head sharply, as if to deny these last trying
days. They had brushed death so often since planeting on
Amazoon. The crash, Bethe's near drowning, the chargefish,
and now this incident—it was as if the gods of this place had
conceived a great hatred for them, or else were giving them
warning . . .

His heart suddenly went cold. So it was a warning, a
preparation for something far worse, far less clean, than any
death with which they had yet been threatened, even the horror
his two comrades had so narrowly avoided this evening.

Fear boiled through him like lava in a living volcano. Islaen
Connor was right. He did know, or sometimes know, when
particularly heavy peril lay before them, or perhaps just before
him. He knew it now, could all but taste the reality, the
inevitability, of it. Amazoon of Indra was a great leech, and
she was going to suck him dry of more than his life, more than
Islaen's life . . .

The former Admiral gripped himself viciously. He forced all
thought momentarily out of his upper mind, made himself
breathe slowly and deeply. Founded or unfounded, this was
panic, and he could not permit himself to be swept by it.
Whatever lay ahead, he had to keep a cool, even head if he was
to be of any use at all either to himself or to his comrades.

The attack was over in the next moment. He was himself

again, his control no longer threatened by the cloud of doom lowering over him, although that cloud pressed ever more heavily down on him. It would not break him now. Only the disaster it portended had the power to do that.

A sharp tugging at her hair roused Islaen. "Bandit, what in space or beyond it is the matter with you?"

She sat up then, fully awake. Her pulse quickened. The gurry knew she was sick. She would not have bothered her without good cause. "What's wrong, love?"

Islaen, help Varn!

Varn! she exclaimed, switching to mental speech. *Is he in trouble?*

No! Yes! Watch over! Unhappy! Scared! Islaen help! With that, she took wing, leaving the Noreenan more puzzled and a great deal more concerned than she had been a moment previously. The Arcturian was in a bad way if Bandit had of her own accord thought it better to withdraw and leave the two humans alone when one of them was in need.

She cast her mind out in search of him. One fear faded at once. Sogan was in no immediate danger, at least. She would have picked up battle readings or the tension that preceded and followed it, even if her consort was screening its nature and his own position from her.

She could be certain of little else. His shields were tightly closed around even the outer portion of his mind.

Varn! Would he hear her at all through those damned defenses?

That worry died as it was born. He might have turned his post over to Bethe Danlo, but he would keep his receptors open to detect potential trouble until he actually lay down. After that, tired as he was, he would have little choice in the matter. His body would demand and claim its own.

His response to her call was instantaneous and sharp. *Islaen? Are you all right?*

Aye.

Sogan reached their sleeping area and hastily pushed aside the gnat netting guarding the two hammocks. He came straight to the woman. She was sitting up, waiting for him. From what he could see of her face in the dim light, she looked well enough, but his alarm did not lessen. The Commando-Colonel was as practiced as he at concealing discomfort. *Why are you awake, my Islaen? Are you in pain? Or feeling worse? Delayed shock . . .*

I'm sound enough, she assured him, relieved by his concern and also touched by it. She knew him well enough that something of the misery gnawing him was apparent to her even from these surface transmissions, yet he had immediately put that aside in his care about her . . .

Her fingers brushed his stern, exhaustion-strained face. *I'm fine. You're the one worrying me right now. —What's happened?*

The man stiffened. *Nothing some sleep . . .*

Put it on freeze, Varn! she snapped impatiently. *Give me credit for having a modicum of perception. There's something riding you, and riding you hard.*

She felt the wall that would sever their minds start to rise, and her eyes flashed. *When you married me, I thought that implied a degree of trust between us.*

His head snapped up as if he had been struck. "It is not that!"

As always, Varn Tarl Sogan reverted to verbal speech when he feared too much of himself might be revealed in what had become their normal mode of communication, but now he glanced uneasily at Jake Karmikel's sleeping form and reluctantly opened the surface portion of his mind once more. Their comrades were too close. None of this must spread beyond them. Had he taken proper care, it would have not gone this far . . .

His eyes lowered. How could he lay this before her?

That was impossible. He would be shamed beyond the repairing if she were to discover the extent of the panic that had swept him.

She must be told something since he had unfortunately somehow managed to betray the fact that he was seriously troubled. He sighed to himself. They had grown so close, he and this former enemy, that it was difficult, aye, and sometimes nigh unto impossible to conceal any strong emotion from her. *I almost believe that you are right, Islaen Connor, that I can see a dark future ahead of us.* His eyes closed in a nearly infinite despair. *I did not dread Mirelle's fungus so powerfully.*

Islaen's breath caught. *What is in store for us?* Or for the war prince himself?

Have I ever been able to tell you that? he asked testily.

No, of course not. I was more wondering than asking. Sorry. She frowned as she studied him. *You're dead spent, Varn. A good part of all this might be stemming from that.*

You think that I am hallucinating, Sogan demanded, *that I am merely working myself up to this?*

No! I wouldn't insult you like that. Her tone gentled. The very fact that he was reacting like this, even with his discomfort at being forced to reveal so much to goad him, told how close he was to the end of his resources, how deeply troubled he actually was. *I do know what your battle with the swarm did to you, though. I knew it then.* This time, it was her eyes that pulled away from his. *A few stings shouldn't have prevented me from doing more to help you, to restore more of that strength to you. Instead, I lay back and let you . . .*

His fingers brushed her lips. *Islaen, do not.* He gave her a tight smile. *You are right. I am about done, and it is likely that I am suffering at least in part from a reaction to that and to everything else Amazoon has thrown at us.* He smiled again, more naturally. *I hope that is the explanation.* Sogan came to his feet. *Trust that I would prefer that answer to the one I just proposed.*

The Arcturian bent and kissed her. *You need rest yourself, Colonel Connor, and you might as well seek it. Neither of us has any choice but to wait and see what the morning will bring.*

SIXTEEN

A GENTLE TOUCH to her mind brought Islaen Connor into full awareness. Her eyes opened to find Varn standing over her, a steaming mug in his hand.

Sorry we could not allow you to sleep longer, Colonel. —How are you this morning?

She ran a quick test on herself before answering him. *Sound out now, praise the Spirit of Space.*

Her brown eyes fixed on him. *I would've thought you'd be out awhile longer yourself.*

I could use more sleep, he admitted truthfully; she could see that for herself anyway. He shrugged, dismissing the matter. *A few additional minutes would have made no difference.*

And the rest? Islaen asked steadily.

I have recovered, I believe. You were correct about that, as I find you are about most things.

It was only partly a lie. The sense of approaching danger remained but it had receded to the background of his awareness where he could ignore it entirely for the most part and control it readily when it did begin to press him. He need not trouble her with that.

The Arcturian handed her the mug. *Breakfast,* he explained. *Bethe thought you and Jake might still have sore mouths, so she boiled your shares up like this. She claims it is not bad, something like a thick freeze-dried fish soup.*

Islaen tasted the unappetizing-looking liquid gingerly. It was too hot for fast downing, but otherwise, it was palatable enough, especially since she found she was quite hungry. *It's actually better than in its usual form,* she proclaimed. "What do you think, Bandit?"

The gurry took a generous sip and declared it good, but she preferred the feel of solid crumbs in her bill. This was no Anathi nectar or some other liquid treat.

The Noreenan took another drink. *How's Jake?* she asked.

He seems to be all right as well. He is over there with Bethe.

Sogan frowned, wondering how true his comrades' apparent recovery actually was. *We two will dismantle the camp and stow the gear, but we will not be able to work alone once we are back out on the river. —We could wait here another day,* he added tentatively.

The Commando-Colonel sent her mind out to Karmikel. *That won't be necessary,* she told him after a moment. *Both of us are fine now and as ready as you to manage the boat.*

That did not mean she looked forward to the job. A repetition of the previous day's labor was not an appealing prospect, and she well knew that conditions on the Maiden would only grow worse until the river finally ceased to exist as a separate entity.

At least, there would come an end to it, she thought. Unless fortune went badly against them or their information, which had proven accurate thus far, was dead wrong, they should win through to the Matron before midday. After that, they should have a much easier time of it until they had to begin the final, overland stage of their journey.

Islaen clung to that hope as the day progressed. She had not been wrong in assuming that the work would be heavier today. The currents grew wilder and stronger as the off-worlders drew ever nearer to Amazoon's greatest river, and although they were not again forced to quit the boat, they did encounter on several occasions fast, rough water that demanded all of their skill and strength. All four of them were well weary before the morning was half spent, but they doggedly kept on, breaking off only often enough to insure that they would continue to be able to respond as they must to the demands of their journey.

Their progress was slow, but an hour before midday, the Maiden turned a sharp bend, and a vast expanse of water lay before them. There was a battle of currents as the smaller river pushed perpendicularly into the larger and for some little while afterward, then they were floating serenely, free of effort and turmoil.

For the first few minutes the guerrillas remained in place, stiffly alert, as if they could not accept that this was more than the most temporary respite, a prelude to some exceptional difficulty. After that they relaxed. The need for vigilance was not quite ended. It would always be necessary to man the paddles to correct a sudden bad side shift or unfavorable drift and to bring them through the sections of turbulent water still to be encountered now and then, but two of their number were sufficient to handle that task, leaving their companions at liberty to rest and to observe the world around them.

Varn Tarl Sogan looked about him, for the first time truly able to study Amazoon's river and riverside communities instead of merely scanning for potential foes.

The Matron was aptly named. This was a stately and magnificent waterway, impressive even this far north, before it came into its full size. It was already more than a mile across and deep in proportion, and its waters flowed freely and quite rapidly considering the flatness of the lands through which it ran. In color, it was dark with the sediment it carried, the legacy of the river systems already swelling it and of the wealth of decomposing plant material from its own bed and surface and the banks on either side.

Because the river was so broad, the sky was clearly visible, a gray ceiling perpetually heavy with the seeds of rain. The Commandos hugged the right bank, keeping well under the overhang of the great trees. There was little real likelihood that their enemies would be sending out airborne scouting parties, but none of the four had survived this long by ignoring any possible source of peril.

The war prince was glad of the respite and the chance it gave him to observe. Although the bank superficially resembled the tangle he had come to know along the shores of the Maiden, he quickly came to realize that this was much lusher, much richer in the vigor and variety of the life forms it supported thanks to the increased amount of light permitted to reach the surface by the river's breadth.

He was very aware of the proximity of larger, more highly evolved creatures now that he had the leisure to seek them out. By ignoring the multitude of marginal readings, he confirmed for himself that Amazoon of Indra was truly a planet of birds and of other tree-dwelling species, and with his talent to help direct his less practiced eyes, he was able to glimpse many of them, although the majority were far too high, concealed in the leaves of the canopy trees three to four hundred feet above.

The Matron itself was a living realm, rich, fruitful, and ever-changing. Plants grew in thick profusion wherever the bottom was close enough to the surface to give them sufficient light, and they, in turn, enriched the water with oxygen and provided shelter and grazing for a vast animal populace.

Again, Sogan ignored the familiar flood of data from insects and like things and concentrated on other readings. As was to be expected, those of reptiles, amphibians, and fish were the most numerous by a great margin, but there were birds that swam and dove and several kinds of mammals wholly or partly tied to the water as well. To his regret, the latter creatures were invariably shy, and he was not fortunate enough to see any of them even momentarily.

The reptiles he sighted frequently, but they did not make particularly comforting viewing. They were more or less the same types as those inhabiting the Maiden, but there were many more of them, and they were on the average larger. Some of them were very much larger.

The amphibians were more numerous. A few, particularly one hard-shelled variety, were large enough to be potentially threatening should a big specimen rise suddenly under the boat at the wrong moment, but chiefly, their interest lay in their astounding variety of forms and adaptations, that and the brilliant colors sported by many.

Fish teemed in the vast aquatic world beneath. The Arcturian honestly regretted that they must remain invisible to him, that he could not put on underwater gear and visit them in their own realm. A large portion of them were reputed to possess great beauty, with vivid, boldly patterned coloration and oddly formed bodies to inspire fascination and excitement. It would have been a real pleasure to see them . . .

Varn caught himself nodding. He fought sleep for a moment but in the end surrendered to it. He would be better for the rest, and Amazoon's gods only knew what might crop up before he had a chance like this again.

* * *

The war prince was primarily aware of a scent, a subtle, haunting perfume that seemed to fill all the universe.

Was this death, then, he wondered. Had he somehow gained entrance to his race's chief paradise after all, despite his disgrace and the mutation that made him a pariah among his own?

A soft, merry laugh sounded in his mind. *Most paradises are rather cooler than this, I think.*

He flushed scarlet. *Witch! Stay out of a man's private thoughts!*

Another, even more amused laugh answered that, and his lips curved despite himself in response to it.

Sogan's eyes opened. He was lying wedged between the baggage where he had drifted off. His head was now resting on Islaen's lap, and a length of gnat netting was stretched over him. One of the tarps looked as if it had just been folded back; it was wet, indicating that he had missed at least a brief shower, and a heavy one.

Did you sleep well? the Colonel asked, smiling down at him.

Aye. His eyes caught hers, then traveled the rest of her fair, exquisitely chiseled face. His fingers reached up to caress her cheek. *You are so beautiful, Islaen Connor,* he said very softly. *In my awareness of everything else you are, I often overlook that.*

I'm a grubby beauty right now, she answered, but she let him feel the full of her pleasure. It delighted her to please this man. She loved him far too much not to want to be attractive in his eyes.

Varn's hand dropped reluctantly. The crowded boat was hardly the place for this. *That perfume?*

The trees on either side. It's from them, too, not just the flowers, or so it seems. At least, we passed a stand a while back that wasn't even in bud, and the scent was every bit as strong.

He sat up, flexing cramped muscles in an effort to work the kinks out of them. *How long was I out?*

Almost three hours.

Space!

Jake Karmikel heard him move and turned around. "Awake at last, Admiral? —Good! You two owe Bethe and me a turn."

Varn missed lunch!

"That is all right, Bandit," Sogan responded sternly. "It will not be long before we break for the night. I can eat then. It is more important for me to help our friends now."

Nooo!

The Commando-Sergeant laughed at the tone of the whistle accompanying that protest. "Eat, Admiral. Please! I'll be feeling guilty for the rest of the day if I'm responsible for depriving her of a snack."

The gurry's feathers extended until her size seemed to double. *Bandit's taking care of Varn!*

"We know you are, love," Islaen said hastily, smoothing down the soft feathers. "Bethe was only teasing. Don't worry. Varn will have his share before he relieves Jake."

The demands made by the river and boat were no longer such that Sogan was unable to devote part of his attention to the world around him even when he took his place at the oars. He was glad of that easing of pressure. Even the small part of her that he had seen before dropping off to sleep was more than sufficient proof that this was a planet worthy of a lot deeper study than he would ever have the chance to give her. Every opportunity to do so was to be cherished and used.

The trees themselves were fascinating, apart from the animal life they housed and supported. He saw some bearing flowers or fruit directly on their trunks. Others had tall spires rising skyward from their broad buttresses, living snorkels to give the plants air during that part of the wet season when the Matron overflowed its banks, inundating miles of the jungle floor on either side. More solved that problem by sending down roots from above. In some species, these formed trunks in their own right once they touched the ground so that a single complex eventually covered yards of ground.

Several times, he spotted vines so heavily in flower that they looked like ropes of blossoms descending from the canopy. As they passed nearer than usual to one of these, he saw flashes of iridescence darting and hovering around the blooms.

Islaen noticed them as well. She peered closely at them, but they were too distant for her to get a good look at them. *Butterflies?* she asked.

Probably. His thoughts reached out and found minds on a higher plane than that. *Birds! Very small birds*.

They must be exquisite up close.

The Arcturian looked at her. There was such wistfulness in that.

He recalled suddenly how he had brought the little junner to Bethe Danlo on Anath of Algola, and once more, he sent his mind out, this time calling.

The response was immediate. Several motes of living light left the flowers and descended to the boat, where they hovered around Islaen and him.

Both humans almost ceased to breathe, so held were they by the minute creatures. The little birds were unbelievably tiny, not quite as large as the outer joint of the man's thumb. Their bodies were slender and their bills long to give access to the nectar pools in deep-throated blooms. The feathers were fabulously iridescent and of an almost indescribable true golden color.

Encouraged by this latest proof of his ability to work with Amazoonan animals, he sought farther and discovered similar touches at every level, apparently wherever seemingly white flowers that were actually strong in ultraviolet hues were to be found. Some of these, too, he drew to them.

Each was a miniature wonder perfectly adapted to its own particular location in its many-storied world, but both he and the Noreenan woman were most deeply held by the denizens of the high canopy, which were to their minds the fairest of all. These little birds were bicolored, green on the back, blue or gray beneath so that they would blend with the leaves should a potential predator pass overhead or with the sky in the eyes of a lower-placed enemy.

At last, he reluctantly released them, not wanting to hold them away from their own places too long.

Varn glanced at his other companions and found that they had been watching with the same rapture Islaen Connor had shown.

Jake released a long, deep breath. "Admiral," he said softly. "I'd give my *Jovian Moon* and ten years of my life to be able to do that."

Sogan looked at him for a moment, then his eyes lowered pensively to the paddle in his hands.

He had never considered his power in this light, as something others would genuinely envy and desire. Islaen did, of course, but he had believed that to be chiefly due to her love for nearly all animal life and to the unpleasantness of so many human contacts. For his own part, he had always regarded it as merely useful or, at best, as a path to desirable knowledge. He had derived pleasure from his consort's and other comrades' enjoyment in some of the things he could do with it, but that it could be a direct source of delight for himself . . . He had not permitted himself to appreciate that aspect of it, not consciously at any rate.

The war prince had to postpone his testing of that newfound potential. Despite the beauty of the tiny nectar sippers and his interest in the rest of Amazoon's life, Varn Tarl Sogan had kept the better part of his awareness on his responsibility for the boat and their lives. He never lowered his consciousness of conditions on the river, and he responded instantly now, as did the Commando-Colonel, when those conditions altered suddenly.

The Matron had encountered a long shelf of extremely hard rock. The great watercourse had over the millennia chiseled a channel through it, but that path was somewhat narrower and more confining than its usual bed, and considerable turmoil was generated in the process of forcing its way through the place.

For more than five miles, the off-worlders struggled with the river. The danger was never immediate, not as it had been on much of the Maiden, but neither could they relax their efforts even momentarily, or they would rapidly have found themselves facing a less easily managed situation.

At last, it was over. As abruptly as the initial change had occurred, so did the Matron return to more normal lowland soil and to its former mild nature.

Islaen and the former Admiral set their oars at rest, and their companions put theirs aside, all in open relief.

Bandit perched on the rail. Her bright eyes darted from one to the other of her humans. *Islaen and Varn, stay working!*

She looked so superior and self-important that the Colonel poked her gently with her finger. "You wouldn't be a bit jealous, would you, love, afraid Varn'll call down more pretty little birds?"

No! Islaen and Varn like animals, love Bandit!

"A sound distinction, small one," Sogan said. He felt no surprise that the gurry was capable of making it. She might have trouble comprehending why some humans turned renegade for gain—Jade of Kuan Yin's rare killers were all afflicted by a deadly madness and were incapable of controlling their need to slay—but a matter of affection, she understood readily.

The Arcturian frowned when he did resume his observations once more. Nothing was precisely wrong from what he could detect, but a change of some sort had definitely taken place.

It was not with the land. The readings from the creatures of the trees and tangle were just about the same as they had been.

The river then.

His dark eyes narrowed. Very obviously the river. The life it held remained rich in numbers, but the mix of species, the variety of mental transmissions, appeared to be gone.

It was instantly apparent what had happened to the Matron's most dramatic residents. The reptiles and amphibians, large and small, lined the banks, sometimes clambering two and three deep on top of one another. Several raised large heads to look at the human party, and a couple opened powerful, sharp-toothed jaws, but none made any effort to return to the water. He shivered slightly within his mind. Even with his ability to control their actions, or partly control them, he was glad neither he nor any of his comrades had been compelled to venture into a stream so heavily inhabited by the magnificent, deadly hunters.

The birds and mammals had also departed their usual haunts for the branches and secluded spaces of the tangle.

What of the things powerless to leave the river?

Sogan sought for them. The marginal contacts, most of them from very small beasts, were there, albeit oddly quiet. So, too, were those of the animals living in the heavy silt of the riverbed, though he believed that many had gone deeper than he had felt them reach before.

At first, he imagined the fish population had remained aloof from the most strange exodus but almost at once realized his error. There were many of them below and around the boat, right enough, but they all appeared to be of a single species.

It took some concentrated mental searching filled out by judicious reasoning to figure out where the rest of that population had gone. His thoughts ranged out, seeking familiar contacts. Sogan discovered them, some of them, in a tiny rivulet draining into the Matron, fish seemingly of every description packed so tightly that there was scarcely oxygen for the poor creatures to breathe. Farther seeking up and downriver revealed other inlets similarly filled.

Because a mystery of this magnitude and complexity could conceivably carry heavy significance for his own party, the Arcturian gave his full attention to it.

Suddenly, he realized the boat was slipping into a sideways drift and quickly went back to his oars.

It took several minutes of sharp rowing on his and Islaen's part to get her back on her correct course once more, but at last they were able to set their paddles at rest again.

"Living in the past or the future, Admiral?" Karmikel asked laconically.

"Quiet!" Sogan hissed. The explanation for the mass movement of the Matron's mobile citizens had suddenly come to him, and it chilled the blood in his veins.

The redhead obeyed. He offered no protest as his eyes fixed tensely on the other man.

Varn drew a breath to steady himself. "Sorry, Jake. It is just that we appear to be sitting above a very large school of sawmills . . ."

"Space!" Bethe exclaimed in a whisper. "This is an inflatable boat!"

"Aye," he responded grimly. "That was my thought as well."

Jake rubbed his hand along the tough material of the side. "She was designed for use in Amazoonan rivers," he reminded them. "We should be secure enough."

"Let's not put that to the test, shall we," Islaen Connor said tightly. She turned to her husband. "What's the situation, Varn?"

"They do not realize we are here, or they do not care. They are actively hunting, however." He had felt it several times already, the surge of eagerness and the sudden termination of a life, when the voracious fish had overtaken some victim that had not fled quickly enough at the school's approach. It was not a pleasant sequence to receive, but it aroused no particular sense of horror in him. This was but the eternal battle between

hunter and hunted, and there were reasonable limits to the
scope of it. The whole school certainly did not try to converge
on a single unfortunate mudcrawler or small swimmer falling
within its grasp.

"You did more research on the local wildlife than the rest of
us, Islaen," the demolitions expert said. "What're the chances
of their trying to rip the boat apart?"

"I don't know," the Colonel told her frankly. "Nothing I
read or heard indicated that they pull things off debris, but I'm
not at all eager to put the temptation before them. They like
meat too well when they can get it."

Sawmills were quintessential carnivores in form, but like
many of Amazoon's other creatures, they were omnivorous,
and the bulk of their food was actually vegetable matter. In
fact, it was they, along with several of the larger water
mammal species, that kept the jungle planet's rivers' potentially strangling plant growth in check. Animal food was avidly
sought when it came their way and was to an extent actively
hunted, but a school did not leave the channel of its parent river
or return to a section just scoured in order to pick up a little
additional prey. Grazing was what kept them alive, and
evolution had seen to it that they stuck to it, an adaptation that
permitted Amazoon's other water animals to survive and
flourish in conjunction with them.

The Noreenan woman turned again to Varn. "How big is the
shoal?"

He shook his head. "I cannot give you a count. The fish are
not swimming densely packed, but they extend beyond our
range of vision in front and behind."

She gave a silent whistle. "What do you suggest we do?"

He hesitated. "That is your decision, but for my part, I
would prefer to slow down and let them get well ahead of us.
We do not know precisely what conditions we will meet farther
on, and I do not care for the idea of those sawmills overtaking
us while we are in the water for some reason or another."

"That makes a pair of us," Jake Karmikel muttered loudly
enough for the others to hear him.

His commander nodded. "I think we all agree there. —Very
well, Admiral. We'll follow your suggestion. We'll do it
slowly, though. A too-rapid slowdown or any other odd

behavior on the part of our boat might alert the sawmills to the fact that there's something abnormal about her."

The Federation party remained tense as they gradually dropped back. None of them wanted to hazard a guess as to how long their vessel could actually hold up under a concentrated assault by the sawmills' powerful jaws and razor teeth. There was no need whatsoever to speculate on their fate if they ever found themselves in the river in the midst of the school. That was a given.

A sudden, loud squealing drew their attention to the bank.

Two capa boars were squaring off over a small herd of two adult and two half-grown females. The one who appeared to be the intruder was a fine, fully developed animal, probably a two- or three-year-old that had not yet been able to claim mating rights for himself. The incumbent was also in his prime, at the height of it, and was large for one of the wild species. The newcomer had to be fairly desperate to confront him; usually only aging, ill, or very young boars were so tried once they had established themselves with a herd.

The challenge was a serious one and had progressed beyond the feinting and posturing stage. As they watched, the younger capa lowered his head and drew back his lips so that his short, keen tusks gleamed white against the coarse, brindled hair.

He charged. The other sprang out of the way, flashing hooves and tusks as he moved. With the speed of thought, he drew his own head in a vicious slash across the attacker's side.

The newcomer staggered under the impact, and even from where they watched, the humans could see that the older beast had drawn blood. The incumbent was a veteran of more than one such struggle in his rise to herd leadership, and he followed fast upon his advantage, charging and striking the injured boar a second time.

His target stumbled, and his feet went from him as he was driven unexpectedly back onto the steep slope of the bank. He squealed once as he began to roll, then he struck the water.

There was another squeal, foreshortened and indescribable, like the scream of a damned soul. With horrible suddenness, the capa was gone from sight.

The river churned, literally foamed, first white and in the

next moment scarlet. Seconds after that the motion ceased, and a white skeleton rose to the surface.

The off-worlders' eyes locked on it. They said nothing, nor did they look at one another when they were able to break their gaze away from the stripped bones. Any faint idea they had entertained that the Arcturian might be able to control the school in the event of a mishap had died in the terrifying reality of those few moments. Varn Tarl Sogan had not been able to drive the wasps off in their anger, and he would have no power whatsoever over these fish when the feeding frenzy was on them.

SEVENTEEN

IT SEEMED A fierce long time before Sogan at last told his comrades that the shoal had left them behind, and even with his assurance and the knowledge of sawmills' habits that they had acquired in their preplaneting studies, all of them remained watchful and tense.

At least, this part of their trek would not last too much longer, Islaen Connor thought gratefully as she checked their charts. She studied them carefully this time, more closely than she had previously done. They should be quite near now.

Finally, she folded them and replaced them in her belt's document pouch. "End of the ride, Comrades," she announced. "That's the bend we want up ahead."

It was the closest point to their enemies that they could reach by water. The Matron did come much nearer. In one loop of its convoluted course, it literally backed upon itself in a tight bend that brought it to the very edge of their target clearing, but they had judged right from the start, before the plan for the aerial attack had been accepted and finalized, that it would be suicide to try that approach even under the cover of night. The camp was too well armed and guarded and the assault force too large. Their much-reduced numbers would have made the risks somewhat more acceptable, but not enough so to induce her to alter their course.

She and Sogan, who were at the oars once again, carefully maneuvered their craft close to the shore.

The four guerrillas sat unmoving for several uncomfortable seconds. It would be necessary to go into the river to make the boat fast, and none of them wanted to be the first to attempt that despite the war prince's assurance that the sawmills were now far downstream and no longer any threat.

At last, Varn made himself smile. He steeled himself not to visibly cringe when he hit the water and slipped lightly over the side.

Fear coursed through him in a sickening wave, but it ebbed in the next moment, and he calmly tugged at one of the mooring lines. "Coming, Captain?" he asked, "or must I ask the Sergeant to help me?"

Jake gave him a sour look, but he responded by dropping into the river himself. Blast the man, he thought. Sogan could get himself in hand far too quickly for anyone else's comfort. He had damn well been as nervous as the rest of them. Even an officer of the Arcturian warrior caste could not have escaped that, not after what they had witnessed and with the transmissions Varn himself must have received while it was going on.

Working together, they soon had the vessel fastened. That done, they boarded again to help their companions unload what they would need for the remainder of their journey and then to secure and conceal both the remaining supplies and the boat herself on the ill chance that they might be required for a return voyage.

It was too soon to break for the night even had the Commando-Colonel not been eager to get as close as they could to the intruders that evening. If they made any kind of time whatsoever today, they should be able to reach the clearing early the following day.

Their packs were not quite as brutally heavy now, with the boats and their gear gone from them, but they were bad enough, and the off-worlders sighed inwardly as they shouldered them. They had a long walk ahead of them, and this weight on their backs would make it no easier.

For a while it seemed as though they would not even be able to begin. The vegetation was so dense and wild along the river's edge that they could scarcely penetrate it despite their sharp axes.

To their relief, once they left the great open expanse created by the Matron's course, the dense canopy of the true jungle closed in, and the undergrowth thinned out rapidly until only the ground with its carpeting of thick, darkness-loving moss remained between the trunks of the massive trees. The seasonal flooding enriched the soil beyond the usual wont of such ground, and the covering was far heavier than had been the case in the highlands. The primitive plants retained their characteristic low-growth habits, fortunately, and did not impede walking apart from making some additional care necessary since they masked minor surface irregularities.

With the disappearance of the brush and succulent ground plants, the animals that browsed and grazed on them also retreated. Their absence, in turn, caused the bulk of the small flying things that fed on them to vanish. For the first time since they had entered the vicinity of the Maiden, the Commandos were nearly free of their persecution.

For several moments Varn gloried in his relief, then he stopped short. He had forgotten the masters of Amazoon's treelands.

The leeches were everywhere, making for the Federation party with what almost seemed to be open delight. Along the ground and down tree trunks and vines they came, their rubbery bodies looping as front and rear suckers alternately fastened and released.

His stomach twisted, and he hastily turned from his comrades.

Don't get sick, damn it! Do something!

The Arcturian whirled around. Islaen was staring at the advancing horde. She radiated no fear—their clothing was ample protection—but their numbers, their pulsing, undulating motion, their-eagerness all worked to disgust even one so accepting of nature's ways as the Noreenan Commando-Colonel.

Sogan flung his mind out. There was no reason here, not so much as emotion, that he could work upon. He concentrated on the concepts of nonfood and bad food.

It was difficult work. The creatures he sought to manage were more primitive in mind than the crown wasps had been and lacked entirely the swarming insects' closely binding social organization. They did transmit a kind of basic call alerting others of their kind to the presence of a food source, and he seized upon that, reasoning the opposite signal should exist as well. If he could convince a few of these leeches, maybe only one or a couple of them, that his party's blood was not usable, he might be able to induce the beasts to retreat of their own accord.

Once more, the uncommon strength of his ability to influence Amazoon's creatures aided his efforts. The nearest leeches stopped. They raised up on their rear suckers, then looped backward and returned to their resting places. Those behind them, the entire living flood, followed suit.

Thanks, Varn, Islaen Connor said in some awe, although she did not look at him. She was not proud of her reaction to the creatures.

Thank you. I should not have enjoyed disgracing myself.

Don't be ridiculous, she said sharply. *No one's expected to like every aspect of our business, and this sort of thing's more difficult for you than for the rest of us.*

Aye, he responded bitterly. *I can never quite pull . . .*

Put that rot on freeze! the Colonel snapped. *I won't stand for that kind of debris from any of us. Noreen's a low-tech, agrarian planet, and Jake and I are both well acquainted with animals and their parasites. As for Bethe, she's seen enough knocking around the rim in a small freighter since the day she was born . . .*

While I am a palace-spoiled princeling?

She felt his laughter, the return of his humor and confidence, and tossed her head. *Do they purposely train Arcturians in the fine art of aggravating those around them?*

Only those of us slated for high command, he assured her. *Come on, Colonel, let us make what time we can before our local friends begin to question the suggestion I have passed on to them.*

The war prince had to keep reinforcing the images he had planted at frequent intervals, but the blood suckers continued to leave them alone, and the unit moved through the dimly lit jungle without difficulty from them or major delay.

Even without the attentions of the parasites, it remained an unpleasant journey. The heat and humidity were all but unbearable and sapped their strength and powers of endurance so that their packs seemed heavier with every step. Water constantly fell on them, keeping their clothing drenched until it chafed their skins raw. Twice, it was momentarily cooling, when thunder showers let loose from the overburdened clouds, but chiefly, it was merely tepid, droplets loosened after having been trapped in the thick canopy until they had grown as warm as the muggy air around them.

Jake wiped the mixed sweat and rainwater away from his eyes. "Can you believe people actually chose to live on this steam pit?"

"They made a success of it to judge by their descendents," Islaen pointed out.

"Aye. That's even more incredible."

"They had to be good to dig in here," Bethe Danlo said. She shuddered. "Look at these leeches! They may be keeping back, but the sons're definitely highly interested in us. —How can they exist in such numbers?"

It was more or less a rhetorical question. She knew as well as the others that the animals could grow on only one full meal in a year and reproduce on half that. They could remain healthy on even less. Many probably did perish, but the numerous small, long-legged moss grazers and other ground dwellers were sufficient prey to support the population as it now stood and permit the replacement of those failing to survive.

A surprisingly sharp clap of thunder caused Karmikel to glance at the canopy. He frowned. Sounds should not penetrate the trees that clearly.

Islaen's eyes darkened as well. "That's not promising," she muttered as she pushed ahead of the others.

They soon caught up to her again when she stopped a short distance farther on, she and the jungle with her. The march of the trees had been brought to an abrupt halt at the edge of a great gash in the erstwhile smooth ground. It was a good mile across and looked to be about forty feet deep, although the densely packed vegetation filling it made that impossible to judge with real accuracy. They could see no end to it in either direction in the short distance before it snaked back under the cover of the trees once more.

An old section of the riverbed, now abandoned by its parent stream. Big, silt-heavy lowland rivers meandered in enormous but sometimes tight curves, and occasionally one of these became so blocked that the water was forced to cut another channel for itself, abandoning that part of its original route entirely. Sometimes rain and flooding sustained the newly formed lake. Sometimes, as appeared to be the case here, most of the liquid either drained away or was sucked up by the plant life rooting in the rich river silt.

The redhead glared at the barrier. He would put a year's credits down that the bottom of that rift was not as dry as it looked from here. Very likely, it was half a swamp, hard to cross and probably filled with every sort of hungry pest Amazoon had managed to produce. Added to that was the rugged climb in and out of it, which would be doubly hard given the weight of their packs and the never-ending heat. There might be a good breeze in this open place at the moment, an accompaniment to the almost-ceaseless thunder, but there was not a hope that it would penetrate the vegetation, even were it not a short-lived phenomenon.

"Can we go around it?" he asked his commander. Islaen did not seem surprised, and he guessed, correctly, that she had been aware of the old streambed from her study of the maps. The rest of them had not gone over them closely since they had decided upon their course.

"No. This isn't a mere loop but a complete alteration in course. It runs fifty miles in one direction and nearly thirty in the other."

He sighed. "I was afraid you'd say that. We might as well start climbing, I suppose."

"Not here, we won't. Those are nettle trees down there, or nettle bushes, rather, which is even worse for us."

She saw that her companions did not understand. "They're rare in the north except in odd sites like this, and there was only a paragraph on them in the back of our notes. Fortunately, it was well illustrated.

"That riverbed holds water far better than the land up here. It probably stays completely flooded much longer as well, and that fact plus its considerably richer soil and its access to light has created another ecosystem. It actually discourages the trees native to the rest of the area and has encouraged colonization by other species normally scarce to or absent from this region, albeit in a somewhat stunted form in the case of real southerners like those lads.

"They're true equivalents of Noreen's herb nettles, but their venom's even stronger, and the carrier hairs'll go through anything short of our boots and then stay active until they decay or are removed. A bad dose can incapacitate a person for days, and it apparently doesn't take much to do it. They're so virulent, in fact, that even the crown wasps tend to avoid areas where they dominate the vegetation mix."

Karmikel examined the plants closely as much out of embarrassment as curiosity. He had believed he had studied those reports thoroughly, and the fact that their other two comrades had missed this as completely as he was no comfort. "Blast our way through?" he asked tentatively.

"With what?" the demolitions expert interjected irritably. "We don't have that amount of explosives with us. We couldn't do it if we set off the whole lot, and then we'd have nothing left to use on our targets."

"What're we supposed to do, then? Fly?" Jake scowled at the obstacle. "We can hardly blame Salombo for forgetting this. He did plenty well for a dying man, but we're still left in a bind now."

"I do not believe he did forget," Varn Tarl Sogan said after a moment. "Let me see the maps, Islaen."

She gave them to him. He opened them, turning his back to the wind as he did so. "This is plainly marked, and he studied them carefully."

"Why, then . . ." Bethe began.

"He knew he did not have time to tell us everything, and he did not see this as a major hazard or block that he should squander what remained of his strength to warn us against it."

"Varn's right, I think," the Commando-Colonel said slowly. "Simon couldn't know precisely where we'd intersect with it. We've probably just hit a particularly nasty stretch."

"Sounds reasonable," the Sergeant agreed.

Bandit will scout! the gurry exclaimed, eager to be of some concrete service to her comrades again.

"Not in these thunders," the former Admiral told her flatly.

But, Varn . . .

"No. A gust or whirlwind could sweep you or slam you into a tree."

Islaen! she pleaded.

The Noreenan looked from one to the other of them. *She probably could do it, and she'd save us a galaxy of time.*

Even as she spoke, the thunder rumbled again, and a gust powerful enough that she had to brace herself against it blew down the corridor formed by the riverbed.

"No, love," Islaen said decisively. "Varn's rarely wrong when it comes to a question of flight." She glanced at the others. "We'll split up," she told them, "go a mile each way. If neither party finds a route down by then, we'll come back here and wait for the weather to clear and let Bandit at it."

"Good enough," Jake agreed.

"You and Bethe go north. We'll head south. Keep your communicators open. If there's any sign of a path or if you run into problems, let us know."

He gave her a quick salute. "Aye, Colonel. Just bear in mind that goes for you three as well."

EIGHTEEN

Karmikel and the Sergeant had scarcely moved out of sight of their comrades when the threatening storm let loose. It had promised to be a fierce one, and without the canopy to block the sight and mute the sound and the force of the downpour and wind, it proved as savage as the world in whose sky it had formed.

Because they knew it would be short-lived, the off-worlders paused in the partial shelter provided by one of the great trunks bordering the rift to watch the tempest.

Bethe whistled softly. "Praise the Spirit of Space Varn stopped Bandit from flying off into this! The poor little thing would've been blown clear to the equator."

"Our Admiral's paid for his passage on this one, right enough," he agreed.

"We've never had a mission when he didn't," she snapped.

Jake's eyes narrowed. Bethe Danlo always rose like this to the Arcturian's defense, to the point that he sometimes wondered about the actual extent of her feelings for him. He realized full well that the blond spacer would never violate her vow to him, that she had meant every word of it, yet still . . .

He knew better than to bring that up again. She would ream him to within a micrometer of his life, and he might lose her altogether. Bethe deserved better from him, and her pride would not continue to tolerate such doubt on his part.

The Sergeant seemed to guess the bent of his thoughts. She turned on him angrily. "What about me, Jake? Are you surprised when I manage to pull my share? I'm space-trained, too, and I haven't even been with the unit as long as Varn. I'm

certainly nowhere near as strong. Am I nothing more than a
constant burden except when I have to disarm something or set
a tricky charge?"

"No! —Spirit of Space, lass, what set you worrying about
that?"

"How shouldn't I worry?" she countered. "Do you think I
want to see you or one of the others killed because of some
half-finned move on my part?"

"You're an asset to the unit," he declared firmly. "Islaen
wouldn't have taken you on if you weren't. She wouldn't have
dared."

The rain slackened as they were speaking, and in another
couple of minutes, it had stopped entirely.

Jake sighed. No sooner did the storm pass off than the heat
and humidity settled over them again as if it had never lifted.
The misery of this place was unending. "I owe you the tail end
of a honeymoon," he said suddenly. "When this is all over,
we'll go somewhere with an agreeable climate and bake the
memory of this hole out of our souls." He softened then. "I
want you to have some peace and pleasure, Bethe. I need to
give you that. There really is more to this universe than war."

The woman's irritation faded in her acceptance of Jake's
love. She could not but respond to it, and she made herself
smile. "We'll have to do better than we did the last time, my
friend. That tropical paradise turned into a proper disaster."

"No more live volcanoes," he promised.

Bethe's eyes dropped momentarily. She stiffened and shuddered visibly. "Space! Look at these sons! Varn's scarcely out
of sight, and they're on us already."

Karmikel glanced down. Three small leeches were worrying
the tops of his boots, and as many more were at the demolitions
expert's. More were on the way toward them from every
direction. "Go after them," he told her. "I can handle
this . . ."

"No! What kind of irresponsible plasma spine do you think
I am?"

He sighed and backed off fast. "Have it your way, Sergeant
Danlo. Just don't blame me if you find one of the miseries
growing fine and fat dangling from the tip of your pretty little
nose."

"Don't be so almighty superior, Jake Karmikel," Bethe

responded icily. "I might just as easily wind up pulling them off you. There's a whole lot more of you for them to glom onto, after all."

"An unpleasant thought, Sergeant. —Let's go, then, since you insist. We might as well at least make moving targets out of ourselves."

They had not traveled two hundred yards before they came to a stop once more. Bethe's nose wrinkled in disgust. "What in all space is that stink? It smells like something's been flushing its tubes around here for the last century."

"You mightn't be too far off in that," the man told her. "A lot of creatures use urine or feces to scent mark their territories, and many have more specialized glands for secreting even more powerful signature substances."

He began to search the area. Animals engaging in that practice were often predators, and anything responsible for this reek had to be big, yet he did not recall the mention of such a hunter in the material he had studied. There was potential for trouble for his party in that mystery.

He had his answer in a few minutes when he discovered an untidy nest of twigs and dry vegetation stuffed into a crack in a tree trunk. Its builder was big, right enough. That slit would have provided adequate if cramped shelter for Bethe and him, and the tangled mass filled the better part of it.

"Sloppy housekeeping," the Sergeant remarked. "What do you think made it?"

He shrugged. "A rodent of some sort, I'd say, since they dominate the fauna mix here. —Its quarters aren't actually fouled, just the area around, and at that, locals probably wouldn't find the smell all that bad. It's as much unfamiliar to us as anything."

"Why a nest at all? Nothing has to hibernate here, surely, and certainly not on ground level. This place floods once a year and stays flooded for months."

"If it's like many other rodents, it probably litters more than once in that span of time. This could be prepared to receive a family."

The size and openness of the place attested to the builder's lack of fear concerning predators, as did the fact that it felt no need to bury or otherwise conceal its excrement.

"Maybe a lot of little things rather than one large creature made it," she ventured, thinking of some of the unit's more unpleasant past experiences.

"No. Look at the size of its scat. And see this." The Captain had uncovered a smeared track in the damp soil beneath a clump of heavily nibbled brush. It was badly damaged, but the impression of a long foot crowned with fingerlike toes was still apparent.

A rustling of leaves caused them both to whirl. A big animal had pushed through the heavy growth and was frozen, staring at them, not three feet away. It was obviously as surprised as the two humans.

The Amazoonan creature was formed like a dome with a long-snouted, narrow head held close to the ground and a body that rose from that to a maximum height of four feet at its back. It was a third again longer than it was tall, discounting the very long, slender tail, and was a quadruped with the hand-shaped feet common to many rodent species throughout the ultrasystem. The fur was short, a dull brown, and looked to be quite soft. The ears were large and round. Its black eyes were small for its size but bright, and the teeth, which were exposed in a soundless snarl, were sharply pointed.

Bethe's lips curled in distaste but also in fear. Things very like this, miniature versions of it, inhabited the back alleys of nearly every port, and every planet where the infestation was heavy or uncontrolled had its tales of bitten drunks. A few had accounts of tragedies, ravaged or slain children.

Slowly so as not to further startle and provoke the beast, she drew her blaster.

Jake's hand covered hers, stopping her from firing. His own weapon was drawn, and he sent a narrow bolt sizzling along the ground in front of the animal.

The rodent jumped, then hastily withdrew into the vegetation once more.

"Let's get out of here," he said tightly.

"On all burners, friend."

The guerrillas put a good distance between themselves and the nest before stopping again.

"That was too close," the demolitions expert declared.

"Not really. I don't think it would've attacked, though fear might've pushed it. There were no young in the nest to spur courage."

"You knew that and didn't tell me?" Bethe Danlo demanded hotly.

"No," he confessed. "I only figured it out after the fact."

She shivered. "I don't like it all the same." She frowned. "Jake, I don't remember any warning about those things. I know I missed the nettle trees, but giant rats are a whole other crew. I'd have spotted even a single line about them."

"They're probably not northern creatures at all," he said thoughtfully. "Our material didn't cover all Amazoon's fauna. It couldn't. An odd one of them or a small colony might come up the riverbed now and then like the plants do. These treelands aren't right for them, apparently, and they don't establish themselves, thus our lack of data about them." Jake's voice became more thoughtful. "They aren't rats, either, or any really close cousins, not by their faces. Port rats have a nasty, sharp look. These don't, to judge by the specimen we saw. It'd have been kind of cute, in fact, if it were small . . ."

"Spirit of Space help me!" the Sergeant exploded. "Noreenans! Varn has my sympathy for a fact. —Was that why you wouldn't let me kill it?"

"Well, the body could attract other things . . ."

Bethe laughed and tossed her head. "Put it on freeze, Captain. You merely couldn't bear to kill an expectant mother, that's all."

"Possibly expectant mother," he corrected, smiling. Karmikel sighed. "Be that as it might, I wish the Admiral had been around. He'd have saved us a scare."

"Aye," his wife agreed. "He'd most likely have told it we were harmless and sent it on its way with no need of fireworks, probably before we'd even half realized it was ever there." She smiled up at him. "Jake Karmikel handled the situation quite efficiently. I, for one, have no complaints whatsoever about his performance."

"I'm delighted to hear you say that, Sergeant."

He shuffled his pack to settle it more comfortably. "We'd better get moving, or we won't cover half our assigned distance."

As they started out, Jake reported the encounter with the big rodent over his communicator.

The Commando-Captain remained silent, thoughtful, after breaking off with his commander. He had done well enough in this instance, but Bethe's courage throughout the incident, even her praise of him, left him uncomfortable about his performance since they had set out from the crash site. It had been hard going, nearly the whole of it, bad for Islaen Connor and himself, worse for their space-trained comrades. Bethe had rightly carried her part, but she would probably have welcomed a little encouragement and support during the long, harsh struggle to win through this far.

She had gotten little enough of that from him, he realized bitterly. He had gone on ahead with the Colonel, secure in his superiority over his less experienced companions and to a degree enjoying it.

Insensitive bastard! He would do well to study their former enemy. Sogan never ignored Islaen Connor's needs. Bethe, too, was a courageous, capable woman slow to whimper under challenge and slower still to ask for the care and concern that should be hers by right. He had often worried over the attraction the Arcturian seemed to hold for her, but it would be no more than he deserved if she did turn to Varn Tarl Sogan if he continued to act, or failed to act, as he had since their troubles here began. He would have to do a galaxy better in the future if he was not to see this relationship he treasured wither and die and be forced to spend the remainder of his life knowing responsibility for its death lay with him alone.

NINETEEN

FOR A WHILE the riverbed presented the same dreary picture, but gradually other vegetation began to show through the once seemingly solid carpet of nettle trees, at first as a mere speckling, then claiming prominence over them.

At last, the Commando-Captain came to a stop. "There! That might serve. What do you think?"

"It looks clear," Bethe agreed doubtfully. She shook her head. "It's awfully steep, Jake, and the nettles push very close along the worst part of it."

"It's also the only place we've seen that looks like it might be a clear path all the way down and across." He studied the narrow way unhappily. The spacer was right in calling it steep, and some of the stinging trees were uncomfortably near. "I'll go down," he said in the end. "If it looks passable, we'll call the others. If not, there's no harm done. We'll just have to keep on looking."

Jake moved carefully. The climb was not exceptionally difficult in itself, but it was challenging, and the conditions under which he was forced to make it were less than ideal. The footing was bad. The recent heavy rains had made rock and soil slick, treacherous support for a poorly placed foot, although the toeholds he found were more than ample when utilized correctly.

He learned to avoid greenery of every sort as completely as possible. The moss, all the ground vegetation, was so wet as to seem almost slimy. It required caution and a great deal of skill not to slide when putting one's weight on it.

Increased physical activity did not lessen any of what he had come to regard as the normal discomforts, either. The flying horde that was part of every open place assaulted him as viciously as any they had encountered in the tangles bordering either the Maiden or the Matron. The leeches were something straight out of a nightmare.

The off-worlder's lips curled in disgust. There was no numbering them, and they were big, on the average at least twice the size of most of those his party had seen in the normal jungle above. Although the nettle trees were inhospitable to most life—the blood suckers cared no more for them than did the better part of Amazoon's other animals—the ground cover and the plants competing with them apparently supported a large warm-blooded population, enough to keep this host reproducing and growing. There were crown wasps around as well, and he had to be constantly on the alert against disturbing any of their nests, but their desire to avoid the stinging trees kept their numbers in sufficient check that the balance of the area was not disturbed. He grimaced. The leech population certainly did not appear to be laboring under any undue pressure from them or from anything else.

He had to watch himself. His clothing provided ample protection, and the heavy coating of repellent he had smeared on his face kept them away from that part of his body, but there was no such defense for his hands. He was using them too constantly and everything he touched was so soaking wet that the cream on them would not remain effective for more than a few minutes. The supply of it that they had been able to salvage from the crash was too limited to permit any such wasting of it.

The Captain swore as he pulled his hand back barely in time to avoid a strike by a particularly large and eager individual. The sons might not be intelligent as humans defined the term, but these seemed almost to stalk him in the manner of higher-level predators. That was not the case in fact, but they sensed the presence of potential prey, and a veritable army of them lined his route waiting for a crack at him.

The one way to prevent them from succeeding was to spot them in time to get out of their way. Nature had fitted them well for their work. They injected an anesthetic when their mouth suckers pierced flesh and then an anticoagulant to keep their victim's blood flowing while they feasted. Any number of them could conceivably drink their fill and drop off of their own accord, and he would be none the wiser until he noticed the small bleeding wounds they left behind.

The monstrosities were not easy to remove before they were ready to go, either, even should they betray themselves. The smallest of them clung to a food source with remarkable tenacity once they succeeded in attaching themselves.

Unfortunately, he had more to occupy him than guarding against this planet's execrable wildlife . . .

Another one! Again, Karmikel yanked his hand away, but this time, he moved too sharply, swung his arm too broadly. It slammed into the soft-looking foliage walling the right side of his path and struck hard against an equally behaired branch.

Immediately such a stab of pain seared the hand and forearm that he feared his heart would stop.

He started to slide. The burning agony rendered the injured arm useless, but he grabbed at a thick, gray root with his left hand.

Jake cried out in revulsion and open fear. Instead of the solid roughness of wood, his fingers closed on a cold, rubbery mass.

He released it in the same moment, but the predator's reflexes were those of instinct, and its response was further hastened by the fact that it had already been poised to strike. The suckered mouth hit the side of his wrist and held fast.

The Noreenan flailed his arm frantically but failed to dislodge the enormous leech even when he slammed it repeatedly against the ground.

His mind abruptly returned to his physical situation. He was slipping downslope. It was too late to stop the fall, but the Commando used his legs to brake and control it as much as possible.

Fortune was with him there. He was already prone, and the remaining distance to the bottom was less than ten feet. He struck with a jolt that jarred him but left him without any significant injuries.

The leech still hung on. It was growing darker but had not yet begun to swell perceptibly. Ignoring the increased pain the movement spread through his right hand and arm, he pulled his blaster, switched it to slay, and burned the horror through as near as he could to its head.

The flesh of the thing shriveled where the bolt struck it, and the bulk of it fell away. Its mouth parts clung to his wrist.

There was no pain in the hand, and he scraped as much of it as he could off on the rocks around. He had to get a look at the wound it had made. To judge from the volume of blood already staining his sleeve and dripping from the numb fingers, it was significant enough to require immediate attention.

His mouth hardened when he at last uncovered it. The leech had nicked the vein. The artery was intact—he would already be beyond helping himself if it were not—but he had to act quickly. The injury was severe and potentially deadly.

Forcing his other hand to move despite the nettle fire rending it, he worked his first-aid kit loose from the belt pouch housing it and pulled the elasticized tourniquet tube from it.

To no avail. The damaged hand would not function finely enough, even with his teeth to help. He could not tighten it effectively.

He looked around him in a desperation that flared into panic. Other leeches, more normally sized but numerous beyond counting, were closing in around him, coming for his exposed flesh from every side.

A flash of blaster fire cleared a space beside him. Bethe Danlo dropped into it, her knees flexed to absorb the impact of her landing. She recovered her balance and fired again, sweeping the blistering ray in a full circle around them. "That'll hold the little bastards off for a bit," she said with grim satisfaction.

She turned to him. "Oh, Jake! —Here, let me get at that." Working quickly, the Sergeant tied off his arm, bringing the bleeding to a stop.

Her eyes widened when she gave her attention to the other one. The hand was flame red and already swollen to more than three times its normal size. The cuff of his tunic bit cruelly into the bloated flesh, and she cut it back to reveal an arm as badly deformed; the garment had offered almost no protection whatsoever against the long, penetrating nettle hairs.

One look at his face, at its pallor and the strain evident in it, told her the agony he was enduring.

She activated the communicator on her left wrist and brought it to her lips. "Islaen?"

"Bethe! Praise the Spirit ruling space! What's happened?"

The sharpness in her voice did not surprise the spacer. The Colonel would have picked up Karmikel's pain and fear and now her own as well. Both she and the Arcturian were probably on their way already. Bethe tensely described the accident and the extent of the redhead's injuries as nearly as she could evaluate them.

Scarcely had she concluded than she had to clear the space around them again. Every millimeter of ground, every leaf and branch that was not a nettle, was pulsing with leeches.

"Get out of here," Jake told her sharply. "They're nothing like this bad above."

"They can't cross my fire," she said more calmly than she felt; there were too many of the things, and she knew she could not hold them off very long before some got by her guard, more than enough to put both of them out of the mission in pretty short order.

"I've got a perfectly good blaster here in my holster."

"Right. You just can't use it."

The reply he started to make ended in a gasp of pain no command of will could smother. She reached out quickly to touch the numb hand. "Hold on, Jake. Our comrades'll be here soon. The renewer'll fix you up fast."

TWENTY

VARN TARL SOGAN came to a stop at the lip of the riverbed. Here was the place their companions had gone down, right enough, he thought, but they must be squarely against the base of the wall. He could get no glimpse of them through the thick vegetation.

Islaen stirred beside him. *I'd best go first,* she said. *If nothing else, I'm smaller. The path down's tight in spots according to Bethe.*

Wait up. —"Bandit, link with me and let me see the route. Once you reach our friends, Islaen can join with us to get a look at Jake's wounds before she examines him herself."

Good thought, Varn, the Commando-Colonel agreed. "Go to it, Bandit."

Yes, Islaen, Varn!

Sogan put his hand on the Noreenan's shoulder to steady himself as all the world seemed suddenly to whirl around him.

His senses stabilized quickly. The gurry was descending very slowly to give him a chance to study the path in detail.

She paused at the place where Karmikel had fallen. A shudder ripped through him when he saw the remnant of the huge leech, but he gripped himself and told the Jadite to move on.

In the next moment he saw his comrades. His throat closed as Bandit swooped low over the host besieging them. So this was a leech grove and this the fate of Amazoon of Indra's sole traitor.

There was no nausea now, no revulsion even, nothing but stark purpose. Bethe Danlo had obviously fired time and again to keep the horde back, but no hand blaster was going to do that forever, and once they reached the humans, those blood suckers would quickly gain access to their vulnerable hands and faces. Even repellent would not stop them long at that point.

His mind lashed out like a bolt of laser fire. His experience with the leeches he had already encountered told him what to do, and almost as soon as his effort began, the Amazoonan host halted and started melting back into the vegetation around them.

His communicator activated. "Aye, Bethe?"

"Thanks, Varn." There was relief in her voice, but fear underlay it. "How long can you hold them, Admiral?"

"Indefinitely. —Islaen is about to link with me. With Bandit's help, she will take a look at Jake and then examine him through her own power. That may tell us how to proceed."

"Hurry," the spacer told him tightly. "He's in a pretty bad way."

Bandit, the former Admiral instructed, *never mind the leeches now. I have them under control. Let us see Jake's hurts.*

Yes, Varn!

His face tightened as the little Jadite moved closer to the injured man. The leech wound was the lesser of the two, and that would require a thorough cleansing to clear out the remaining parts of the creature and the anticoagulant it had injected. The other arm was frightening. They were dealing with poison there, and it was still being inexorably injected by the embedded hairs. He did not know how much the renewer would be able to do with that.

Islaen's mind separated from him as she turned her will to studying the full measure of the damage their comrade had taken.

It was several minutes before the Colonel looked up at him. Her eyes were somber. *It's bad. I doubt our instruments are fine enough to get those hairs out, and we can't just put him to sleep until they decay naturally.*

Will it kill him? he asked bluntly.

Probably not. He's strong, but the pain's intense. He sure as space won't be able to help either us or himself. —Damn

Amazoon of Indra! We can't even stay down there. Between the blood suckers and the flies . . .

I will take care of the leeches, he told her firmly. *We shall have to depend on the repellent and nets for the rest if you judge it best not to move him right away.*

She sighed. *I know, Admiral. I just don't like the way any of this has turned out.*

That makes us a pair, Islaen Connor. —Start, Colonel, since you will probably still insist on taking the lead down.

She gave him a quick smile. *That I shall, my friend.*

Sogan waited until she had gotten a reasonable distance ahead of him before starting himself. He sighed in his heart as he did so, knowing the ordeal that lay ahead of him. He had been able to manage well enough in the normal jungle, but there would be no respite at all below . . .

He tested the strength of the shields he had already raised over his thoughts, then squared his shoulders. The Commando-Colonel had enough to worry her in Karmikel's injuries without allowing her to learn about what should remain a minor, if unpleasant, difficulty of his.

Islaen was already bending over Jake when the war prince reached them. She was working on the leech wound, scrubbing it out with antiseptic from her first-aid kit and a hastily boiled canteen of water. The redhead grimaced as he watched her but did not appear too much distressed. The anesthetic was still active, then.

Sogan bent down beside him as well. "Impressive," he remarked to the other man.

"Aye." He scowled. "This seems to be my mission for running afoul of the local wildlife. Of all the scramble-circuited moves . . ."

"Be quiet, will you," Varn told him.

He looked up. Bethe was returning to the group with a two-foot length of three-inch-thick vine, which she was holding carefully pinched at both ends. "Here it is, Islaen, chuck full of water like you said."

"Good. —You tied off both parts of the vine? It's a handy supply and there's no point in killing off the plant."

"Just as you instructed, Colonel." Her eyes fixed on her husband. "Jake?"

"Coming along," he replied. He tossed his head, restless now with the constant pain and the fever it was raising in him.

Islaen finished her cleaning of the limb at last and took the renewer from her pack. After that, it was but a matter of seconds before the wrist was whole again.

There was no such ready remedy for the grotesquely swollen right hand and arm. There was no remedy at all. She had little hope of being able to remove the nettle hairs piercing it under any conditions; in flesh this bloated, there was no chance whatsoever of doing so.

She stared at the limb helplessly, angry because of her helplessness. Suddenly a thought came to her, and her head snapped around. "Varn, get me that blood sucker's mouth parts, then put the other leeches around here to work on its body over there. I want it impregnated with their saliva. When you think it's ready, fetch it here to me."

He wasted no time with a verbal reply but nodded curtly and set himself to work out and transmit the necessary images.

It took him a while to discover the pattern, more than half an hour, for the dead of their own kind were not their natural prey, but once he had it, the job was done within a matter of minutes. No individual leech stayed with the corpse for more than a couple or three seconds, but there were so impossibly many of them in this place . . .

He picked up the thing and brought it to her, cringing inwardly at the feel of it in his hands.

The woman nodded in satisfaction. "Even bigger than I'd hoped," she remarked. "Split it in half lengthways and put it down here beside me."

She chose a scalpel from her medical kit and stripped away its sterile wrappings. With this, she scored Jake's hand and arm, slicing the reddened flesh every couple of inches along the whole length of the limb. When the last cut was made, she lay the dead leech across it and bound it snugly but not overly tightly with a bandage strip from her kit.

"Let that sit for a while," she said. "With luck, it should numb the pain somewhat and help drain out a good part of the poison. If I can get enough of the swelling down, I might be able to do something about the rest."

Jake's eyes closed. Was he imagining it, or was the fire already beginning to cool just a little?

They opened again. "It can be draining on the move. We've still got time to get across this hole and up the other side before nightfall."

"Forget it, Jake," Islaen Connor told him. "We camp right here until we've seen to you."

"Think again, Colonel. Whatever he says, Sogan isn't going to be able to hold the wildlife off us forever, not in the kind of numbers that exist down here, especially with my blood to whet their appetites. Where'll we be if he gives out? This is one big leech grove, remember? Salombo expected us to go through it in a quick dash, not set up housekeeping."

"I will manage," the former Admiral said coldly.

"All right, Varn," the woman told him. "He has a point. The last I noticed, there were still a few human curbs on your abilities." She felt him stiffen but ignored that. Sogan had been wielding his talent constantly since they had discovered he could manage Amazoon's leeches, and he had pushed himself hard to meet one emergency after another since the crash. There had to be some limit to his strength.

She hesitated as she looked at Karmikel. They would never be able to carry him . . . "Do you think you can make it, Jake?" she asked gently.

"I'll make it. No fear of that." The Noreenan man felt worn out merely by the argument, but he knew he had won and braced himself to press his advantage. If he collapsed en route, so be it. Conditions might be better for a camp farther from the wall, but whether they were or not, he was determined to make the effort. He preferred to go down trying to win his life than to lie here waiting for an army of leeches to drain him dry. "Give me a hand up. We've lost enough time as it is."

TWENTY-ONE

THE ARCTURIAN BORE most of his comrade's weight for the first quarter mile, but after that, Jake began to take more and more responsibility for himself. Sogan was grateful for that, although he gave no outward sign of his relief. The ground was viciously difficult to cross, swampy and choked with low growth. It was necessary to watch constantly where he placed his feet and also to guard against striking any part of a nettle tree. They were not numerous in this area—Karmikel had chosen his path well—but there was always the odd branch waiting to claw at an unwary traveler.

The leeches pressed him hard and continuously. They were, if anything, even more heavily concentrated near the center of the old riverbed than they were at its outer edge, and they seemed far hungrier and more persistent. He had to reach deeper and deeper into himself for the strength to feed the commands he sent out to hold them at bay.

As if that were not wearing enough, he had also to battle the ever-more-violent throbbing in his mind itself, the pulling of the strange scar that was the legacy of the mind duel he had fought with his renegade kinsman in defense of Omrai of Umbar. Even now, the pain was almost blinding and threatened the concentration he needed to maintain in order to control the blood suckers, and he knew he could only expect it to worsen in the long hours ahead.

He strove to ignore it and cursed himself when he could not and it claimed an ever-increasing part of his awareness. The Noreenan Captain was forcing greater and ever greater effort from himself, and he who bore no wound was weakening, threatening to fail in the service his comrades expected and needed from him, the service they trusted him to provide.

Provide for them and for himself. He shuddered despite himself. No member of the Arcturian warrior caste courted death either in battle or by his own hand, but neither did his kind have any inordinate fear of the Grim Commandant. Death under the suckers of Amazoon's leeches was another matter. The thought of it filled him with a chill he once would have considered himself disgraced to own. The idea of Islaen Connor's meeting such a fate, he could not even bring himself to contemplate.

That could well be her end if he did not hold up now. Varn Tarl Sogan willed himself to go on, refusing to yield at all to his weariness or to the blistering pounding behind his temples, although it soon required nearly the full of what the battle against the leeches left of his concentration merely to keep himself moving.

Varn stumbled to a stop in response to the Colonel's unexpected signal and sagged against a tree, scarcely able to force himself to check first that it was insect-free.

He roused himself again in the next instant and made himself take note of the reason for the unscheduled halt.

They had come to the approximate center of the riverbed. A stream bisected it, not a proper river, but more of a ribbon of very liquid mud some ten feet wide. Another ten feet or more of soft muck of uncertain consistency bordered it on either side.

Jake gave a weary sigh beside him. "I don't think this planet likes us a whole lot," he grumbled. "I wonder how deep it is?"

"And what kind of wildlife it houses," Bethe Danlo added with even less enthusiasm.

Sogan smiled. "Perhaps I can answer that last, at least," he said.

He started to search out any creatures dwelling or hunting in the mud stream and its borders but moved too quickly for his already strained senses. The effort sparked a surge of pain so sudden and sharp that he gasped and reeled back against the tree once more.

For the first time since Karmikel had been hurt, the demolitions expert's attention swung away from her husband.

Her small hands closed on Varn's arm with a strength surprising for their size. "Admiral, what's the matter?" she demanded in alarm.

Those few moments were all he had needed to recover himself. "Nothing at all, Sergeant," he responded lightly, forcing himself to smile and straighten as he spoke. He glanced at the muddy soil. "A careless step and a slip."

"Rot!" the woman told him flatly. "Man, your face is gray!"

Islaen spun around. Only now did she realize that his mind had been completely closed to her since they had reached the bottom of the embankment. "Varn?"

The Arcturian frowned. "It's nothing, I said."

That was patently not true.

Varn's head hurts bad!

"Bandit!" he snarled.

The Colonel's heart grew cold. The wound he had taken on Omrai had very nearly killed him, and he had been unable to exercise his talent long-term since then. If that scar ripped open now . . .

Sogan stiffened as he felt her begin to examine him, but he knew there was no blocking or resisting this process and so made himself submit to it.

He winced when she reached the center of his pain, but then his eyes closed in an exquisite relief. Her touch was gentle and almost incredibly soothing. She could not heal everything, no more than she had been able to cure him completely after Aleke's attack, but the sharp edge was soon gone from the headache.

Thanks, he said softly, in some wonder that it did not even hurt to use his mind thus. He had been unable to do so at all for some time after having sustained the original wound.

Varn, why in the name of all the Federation's gods didn't you say something?

What good would it have done? I would still have to go on . . .

I helped you now, and you jolly well won't go on anymore! We'll just have to put up with the local nasties for a while!

We cannot! They are even worse here, many times worse, than they were at the bank. They will be all over us within moments if I stop. Maybe we could get through with minimal

*damage if we were all sound, but Jake cannot manage that kind
of speed.*

What're we supposed to do if you collapse on us? she asked.

That will not happen! He was angry now, at her and more so
at himself. *If I had not been studying myself so carefully since
the duel, the scar would be stretched out by now, and I would
not have to put up with this. As it is, I am just going to have to
endure it, preferably without whining like a menial.*

His pupils narrowed as the throbbing ache returned in full
force, and the woman hastily yielded. *All right, Varn. You're
programming the course, but you'll rest once we regain the
normal jungle. —You'll be in no shape to fight if you don't.*

Assuming the pressure on us eases, he agreed. His eyes
smiled as he accepted her return and the renewal of her healing
touch, but determination firmed within him. Whatever discomfort he might have to carry, this woman was not going to
endure any hardship that it lay in his power to prevent. Most
particularly, he would not permit her to face persecution by the
loathsome creatures engendered by this accursed excuse for a
planet.

The Arcturian obediently swallowed the tablets Islaen
handed him and rested for several minutes, but after that, he
carefully examined the mud flow and its environs. "There is
nothing near that we need fear," he informed his comrades
with satisfaction and also with relief. "I sent several snakes
downstream, but even those would probably not have troubled
us. I found no life forms very far down, either, so I do not think
it is too deep."

"We'll confirm that soon enough," the Commando-Colonel
said, then added. "We'll go across roped, just in case."

Sogan watched as his consort half stepped, half slid into the
main stream. His muscles tensed. If it proved deeper than he
thought, or if it had anything of the nature of quicksand, they
would have to be ready to pull her out fast.

The Noreenan took her time with the crossing. At one point
she sank to her waist, but she had no difficulty and waved them
on when she came to the solid ground on the opposite shore
several minutes later.

Bethe followed her, and then it was the men's turn.

Varn moved to support Jake, but the redhead held back. The

war prince's lips tightened. "Do not give me trouble as well," he growled.

Karmikel glanced uncertainly at Islaen. He yielded when he received her quick nod. He had little choice anyway, he thought. He had improved under her unorthodox treatment, but it was a matter of degree only, and he knew he would not go far unaided, certainly not across that mud.

There was a bad jar as he slid into the stream, and he only partly succeeded in choking back a moan.

"Are you all right?" Sogan asked quickly, automatically adjusting his hold so as to put less pressure on the injured arm.

"I'll do, Admiral. In another day or so, I'll be ready to carry you out of here."

"Not on this voyage, Captain."

The other chuckled. "The fortunes of war may have something to say about that, my friend." He fell silent suddenly. "If there is a war. Even if I were still worth something, we don't have any small army to back us now."

Varn Tarl Sogan said nothing for a moment. His eyes grew dark and bleak, then he recalled himself and shrugged. "We must see those ships before we can decide how to proceed against them. There is no profit in worrying about that part of it at this stage. As for yourself, give Islaen Connor a chance to go to work on you before you plan on sitting this one out."

The stream was the last delay they encountered, but the thick growth made for hard, unpleasant walking, and they were all well tired by the time they reached the farther wall of the old riverbed.

Sogan's heart sank when he saw it. The climb was no challenge in itself, but the bank was sheer enough, and nettle trees lined the whole of the way. "You will have to help," he told Jake. "I cannot bring you up by myself." It shamed him to have to admit that. Karmikel had carried him out of that burned starship on Anath of Algola . . .

The bigger man just smiled. "Hardly, Comrade, with as many pounds as I have on you. —Give me a push now and then. That'll suffice to get me to the top."

TWENTY-TWO

DESPITE HIS ASSURANCE to the contrary and his efforts to make the truth of it, the Noreenan Captain needed considerable aid to scale the embankment, and both men were well spent by the time they dragged themselves over the edge to lay gasping under the first of the great jungle trees.

Islaen knelt beside Varn. When he did not move in response to her coming, she put her arm around his shoulders. She was certain he was beaten, but when he looked up, she saw that was far from the case.

He smiled at her. *The bulk of our hosts have stayed below,* he informed her. *We will not have it so bad from here on, unless we run into another such barrier, that is.*

The Spirit of Space forfend!

The Colonel gave him her hand. He came to his feet reasonably lightly, enough so to reassure her considerably. Still, she was determined that they would break soon, before Sogan and the rest of them were exhausted to the point that they would need a stop of several days to restore themselves. *As soon as we move back far enough to be out of range of these thrice-blasted flies, we'll hunt up a campsite.*

Sogan stiffened. *You wanted to push on* . . .

The woman frowned. *Jake's keeping going on will and Noreenan stubbornness. Do you want to see him drop?*

Am I so small in your eyes?

Sorry, Varn. I'm nearly done, too, I guess.

I was off the charts. He glanced at the other man, who was drinking deeply from the canteen Bethe was holding for him. *What will you be able to do for him, Islaen?*

151

I don't know. I dread having to face that question. It could well be precious little, or maybe nothing at all.

The off-worlders traveled a short distance farther. The swarm of flying things hovering around them decreased dramatically as soon as they left the open place behind, and Islaen was not long in selecting a campsite.

"Varn, Bethe, set up the hammocks while I take a look at Jake."

The Colonel cut away the much-dehydrated leech and rinsed off the last remnants of it.

Her lips tightened. The swelling was greatly reduced, and she could readily see the tiny white dots, all too many of them, where the nettle hairs had penetrated and remained within his flesh. Her head lowered. Her fears had been all too well founded. It was hopeless. There was nothing in their medical gear nearly fine enough to draw these out.

Her eyes avoided Karmikel's. How was she to tell him that she could be of no use to him whatsoever, that he would have to wait for nature to take its course or until they reached a proper hospital before he could expect any relief?

The gurry fluttered to her hand and peered intently at the reddened limb.

She gave a sharp whistle. *Bandit can help!*

The Jadite hopped to Jake's arm. Her talons were keen as needles and functioned as delicately as precision tools. They pressed into the numbed flesh, and in the next moment, she bent her head to retrieve the hair she had exposed.

Varn whirled around as pain ripped into him even as it tore her bill and tongue. "Bandit, stop that! You are getting hurt!"

He was beside her in a couple of strides, but not before she had seared herself again drawing out another of the hairs. "Stop it, little fool!"

He reached out to forcibly pull her away but yanked his hand back with a gasp as her claws raked it.

Bandit help Jake!

Let her at it, Varn, Islaen said quickly. *She's the only one who can do anything for him. —She's scored you proper. Come on. I'll see to your hand.*

She looked at the five claw marks, all of them bleeding freely. *I'm sorry, Varn,* she said softly. The cuts were nothing in themselves, but the war prince loved Bandit so much . . .

Sogan shrugged. *Wash it out well before you use the renewer. The little witch scraped in some of that poison.*

The woman grimaced. *That hurts.*

Aye. His body tensed. *She is suffering terribly, Islaen.*

I know.

She irrigated the wounds and closed them with the renewer. After that, she returned to Jake, trying to close her mind to what the gurry was enduring.

Karmikel looked up at her in stark misery. He, too, loved Bandit. "There's no other way?"

"No."

"I'd feel better if I could be taking a lot more of the same," he told her tightly.

"Don't you think we all would?" she asked bitterly.

Bandit worked her way down the limb, whimpering sometimes but not faltering until she had carefully laid the last nettle hair on the carcass of the dead leech and watched Islaen flame it with her blaster to eliminate any chance of their picking up one of the accursed things as they moved about the campsite.

She flew to the Colonel. *Islaen help Bandit? Bill hurts!*

"I'll try, love."

The woman used a syringe to wash the bill and tongue. When she had removed as much of the venom as she could, she applied a liberal coating of anesthetic cream, the strongest medication she dared use on the tiny creature. It would not numb the pain completely, but it would ease it considerably.

Bethe had helped Jake to his hammock by the time their commander could give her attention back to him. "Put him out, Islaen?" the spacer asked, raising the needle she had already prepared.

"Aye. A good night's sleep's the best medicine we can give him right now."

The Arcturian's eyes were shut, but they opened at Islaen's approach. *How is Jake?*

Asleep now. He should be a new man by morning.

I hope you are right, he said doubtfully. *He did not need a second dose of venom after that round with the crown wasps.*

We've lucked out, I think, praise the Spirit ruling space.

—What about yourself? she asked more gently.

I would give a lot of credits right now for a long session under the Maid's *showers. —By all the old gods, I would have cashiered any man under my command who permitted himself to fall into this state!*

She smiled. *You were your equivalent of Regular Navy then, Admiral, and such things as the condition of one's uniform was of some importance. You're a Commando now.*

I was referring to my person, not my clothing.

That's just another basic disadvantage of a guerrilla's life, I'm afraid.

Islaen lay her hand on his forehead.

He moved his head away. *Stop fussing, Colonel. There is no fever.*

None, she agreed. She almost wished that there were. He felt cold, his sweat clammy.

Bandit perched beside his head. She licked his cheek despite the soreness of her tongue. *Bandit's sorry to hurt Varn!*

Sogan stroked her gently. "You're not to be blamed for being brave, small one. You were right. I just hated to see you in pain."

Bandit knows! Varn loves Bandit! She rubbed her head against him. *Bandit's tired! Varn, too!*

"You both settle down for the night," Islaen ordered.

Something in her tone caused Varn to raise his head. His eyes narrowed when he saw the needle she was readying. *I have no need of that,* he said sharply.

A light dose. You'll be able to wake if something happens, but I want you to sleep the full night out if all stays quiet.

What about the leeches?

Like I told you earlier, we have the nets and tarps and our clothes. It may not be any fun, but we'll manage.

The Noreenan waited with him until the shot took effect, then withdrew to finish the work of setting up the camp.

Bethe joined her. "Asleep?"

"Aye, with a little chemical help. He needs that more than a share of rations tonight. —Let's light our burners. I want to be under nets before the local wildlife starts getting interested in us again."

The demolitions expert bit down on her lip. "What're we going to do Islaen? With three of us out . . ."

The Commando-Colonel sighed wearily. "We pray, Comrade. They should all sleep the bulk of this off." Her voice turned grim. "If they don't, we'll have had one hell of a trek for nothing. There'll be nothing for it but to scrub the whole plan, such as we have of one."

TWENTY-THREE

VARN TARL SOGAN woke slowly. He was conscious of a strong, heavy smell and a muted light behind his eyelids. There were no camp sounds, and he gratefully started to will himself back to sleep until true morning should come, but Bandit stirred beside him. *Varn's awake! Good! Send leeches away!*

His eyes opened. All the net above him, and probably the hammock beneath as well, was one solid mass of quivering living flesh. "Space!" he whispered, and for one instant, he longed passionately for the immaculate bridge of his flagship with the best crew in the Empire at ready to do his will and the clean, cool expanse of interstellar space before him, far from the heat and filth and horror of Amazoon of Indra.

His mind flowed out, and in the next moment, the blood suckers began to fall back. Within minutes, he had to peer hard into the surrounding treelands to spy out any of them.

Thanks, Varn. Islaen Connor's relief was apparent and sharp enough that he felt guilty for having slept so long and worse still for momentarily wallowing in self-pity while she had needed his help, for yielding at all to the yearning for that which could never again be.

He made a show of stretching. *Our patient is recovered this morning?*

Jake's grumbling at the leech for not striking the nettled hand in the first place and sparing him the need of wearing its corpse for an armlet.

He will survive, he commented dryly. He tickled the gurry in the sensitive place where bill and feathers joined. "I can see that our brave little comrade here is herself as well."

The hen purred loudly. *Yes! Bandit's fine now! Varn, too, almost!*

Sogan gave her a poke with his finger. "I am well enough to deal with you if you do not keep quiet!"

She squawked. *But, Varn . . .*

Islaen laughed. "Quiet, you two! You're enough to addle anyone!"

Her eyes fixed on her husband. *Varn?*

The man sighed patiently. *I am well enough. Still a bit tired, but there is nothing more dramatic than that wrong with me.* He was not about to call attention to the shadow headache already building behind his eyes. A couple of the tablets he knew she would press on him would take care of that.

He studied her closely. *You look tired yourself, my Islaen. You and Bethe divided the watch?*

We managed.

The Commando-Colonel glanced over her shoulder and straightened. Their two companions were coming toward them, obviously ready to resume their business once more.

Varn hastily sat up and reached for the boots Islaen had drawn off him after the soporific had taken full hold. If their maps continued to be as accurate as they had thus far proven, they should reach the intruders' clearing before nightfall, baring any further unanticipated challenges.

Islaen spread out the charts and repeated the data the Amazoonans had been able to gather, although they knew it all well enough already.

"There's not a whole lot we can do in terms of concrete planning," she concluded. "No one was able to get close to those ships to give us a real account of them, and even if they had, things change over a matter of days. We could be facing three ships or more or less. If our luck has really soured, they could all have lifted."

Her voice was grim as she said that last, and the statement was somberly received. That would mean the arms had been transferred to their ultimate buyer, and once they were, they would not surface again until they were put to the use for which they had been taken. At that point, the unfortunate populace of some planet would pay the price for their failure.

"We'll have to assume they'll be there," Bethe Danlo said, "but what in space are we going to do with them? I know military miracles are supposed to be our forte, but we were counting on those lasers, not to mention a backup force to help keep our opponents busy while we were using them."

The auburn-haired woman answered with a cold smile. "We came away with our personal gear, friend, and that includes our explosives. Commandos even less well supplied faced heavier odds than this during the War and rarely failed to take out their targets. Once we get into that camp tonight, I'll just about guarantee that neither arms nor starships will see space again."

"Assuming nothing else goes wrong," Jake added. Over-confidence had no place in their work; on Amazoon of Indra, it was all but ludicrous.

"Aye," Islaen agreed slowly, accepting the rebuke. "That applies to any mission, and it's a still greater factor here. We won't so much as be able to make a solid counterplan until we actually see the base."

Bandit could scout!

"No," the former Admiral commanded quickly, before she could take wing and be gone. "It is too far yet. This is not Anath where we had a fixed camp. Separate from us, and we might not be able to connect again quickly enough, mind link or none." He did not want her caught up, alone and helpless, in anything he might have to start . . .

Bandit's careful! Will find friends!

Sogan flushed, embarrassed by this third display of his feeling for the little Jadite, his need to guard her, in so short a span of time.

To his surprise, his consort nodded. "There are no forests on Jade, love. You aren't used to dealing with large treelands, and it'd be plaguey easy to get lost in this mess for anyone. Stay with us awhile longer. We'll almost certainly have to send you out when we get closer."

There was a different mood on all the Federation guerrillas when they set out. With less than a day's march between them and their enemies, they moved cautiously, on the alert for any sign of potential trouble.

Varn could use only a portion of his mind to control the leeches now, although neither could he abandon that war entirely. The bulk of his effort was concentrated on ranging the jungle around them, touching with the life forms he found and seeking any hint of human penetration.

Islaen, too, was drawing on her talent, sending her thoughts out in search of her own species. Sometimes, she linked briefly with Varn, but usually each of them worked alone, ever looking for signs that would tell them the danger they had come to Amazoon to challenge was near.

The former Admiral was just as pleased to work by himself on this occasion. With all the rest of the demands being made on his mental and physical powers, it was difficult to screen his inner thoughts when they did link for a few moments, and those were of such a nature that he had no wish to share them with his consort.

Their journey through that leech grove of a dried riverbed had finished him with Amazoon of Indra. He hated the planet. All he wanted now was to complete their mission quickly and get away from her. Whether he would still be able to consider himself an officer, or human at all . . .

Sogan angrily drove that thought out of his mind. It came too often since that grim scenario of the course he might be compelled to follow had first thrust itself into his consciousness. His eyes closed. He did not want it. The Spirit of Space knew how violently he recoiled from a deed that would damn him utterly in his own eyes and in those of these comrades he had come to love above all the rest of the universe, who were his universe.

The war prince sternly gripped himself. It would not come to that. What he had envisioned was the blackest possible pivotal situation and the dire solution required to counter it. They would actually find something entirely different. They would either arrive too late, or they would handle their enemies by conventional means, as far as that term could be applied to any Commando action. Even if it did come to pass that he had to strike in the manner he feared, he had the strength and power to see that it did not become the massacre he shrank from contemplating. Surely, he could trust his ability to control the effects of his call well enough that whatever he started would not explode into a holocaust nothing human could halt or turn.

That reasoning, forced by his will as it was, reassured him, and Varn sighed in relief. He was miserable enough physically without permitting himself to be tormented by shadows as well. He smiled wryly. A guerrilla leader, any officer, needed an ample and active imagination, but there were times in plenty when it was nothing short of an outright curse.

He was last in the line of march again, and Sogan let himself drop back a few more paces. He wanted to stop for a while, to rest and think, simply to be by himself, but privacy was a luxury rarely to be had in this work he had taken upon himself. This was the best he was going to be able to manage for some time to come.

There could be no thought of drifting off into some mental realm of his own anyway. The task of scanning the jungle around him would have been enough in itself to forbid it, and he was not even free to devote himself exclusively to that. His never-ending battle to keep the leeches at bay demanded much of his attention and sapped a good part of his energy, as did the need to watch where he was walking. As long as he precisely followed his comrades' trail, he was fine. The two leaders were studying where they were going. If he should step aside without giving a proper look to his surroundings, though, he could find himself in trouble. Both Salombo and their own briefing material had warned of a danger that infested this stretch of the jungle.

The sources of it were easy enough to spot. His eyes fixed one even as he thought of them. It was a plant, a relatively small specimen of its kind that rose three feet out of the ground and then stopping abruptly, giving the impression of a broken stump. A basin formed of specially adapted leaves extended an equal breadth and depth from its base. In color, it was a leprous greenish-white and formed an ugly contrast to the rich red-brown of the trunk near which it was growing.

The moss-bed flooring of the forest grew particularly luxuriantly in a wide circle around it. That would have to be the case, he thought, since the small plants were never grazed down.

He studied the seeming stump as closely as he could in passing. The thing was carnivorous, or omnivorous, rather, since it just as readily accepted plant material falling into its waiting basin, although it did so only passively. Some incomprehensible instinct warned it not to seek food from the supporting, sheltering trees or sweep up any of the debris falling from them unless it dropped directly into its maw, as if it consciously realized the decay of such material was essential to replenish the ground and nourish both the trees and its own weak root system.

Other food it did take, literally. There was no question of intelligence, but these strange plants did not meekly wait for prey to drop into them or set lures to draw small things to them. They hunted, actively and successfully.

Outwardly, the squat plant seemed to stand alone, a complete, ugly unit, but what was visible here was only the core of an efficient, far-reaching assault network. The roots, so poor at the mundane work of drawing nutrients from the soil, spread in a vast lace work throughout the ground around the base plant, periodically sending up runners, not to form young plants of the same physical type but seeming to assume the personality of vines that climbed nearby trees and dangled over their lower branches much in the manner of the conventional growth they resembled. So they stayed and lived until some creature of a size sufficient to activate their sensors passed near or below one of them.

In that instant the alerted tendril leaped to fulfill its purpose, dropping down and whipping about its victim with unrelenting and irresistible force, crushing it with such power that it was usually a corpse and nearly inevitably a senseless body that it cast into the basin of the core plant, there to be dissolved in the virulent acid it contained and absorbed through the membranes of the cup leaves.

Most victims were small by human standards, the largest commonly being little moss grazers or, occasionally, something plucked from the canopy, but large specimens had killed men in the past and had done it so quickly that their horrified comrades had been unable to act in time to save them.

Varn Tarl Sogan's expression remained impassive. Potentially deadly as they were, the hunter plants did not arouse any inordinate dread or disgust in him. They were a peril unique to Amazoon of Indra, one meriting great caution on the part of his unit, but to his mind, they were no more than that. There was nothing loathsome about them in or of themselves.

Not alone, at least. They were patently successful and had infiltrated every part of the planet's treelands meeting their rather stringent requirements. The thought of encountering a major grove of them sent a chill through the deepest part of him.

The former Admiral quelled that easily enough. There was no fear of that. It would not happen, because it could not. The plants were strictly solitary. Too many in one place would have rapidly depleted the prey it contained, working the destruction of all, and so nature had moved to assure that this would not occur. The far-ranging roots secreted a substance inimical to others of their kind, and only when injury or age, disease or starvation, felled an incumbent plant could another of its kind rise up and prosper within its former sphere of influence.

That successor would almost inevitably be one of the dead plant's own offspring, the first to touch the soil of the numerous tendrils that raced groundward in response to some genetic trigger. As soon as it buried itself, it put out roots of its own and severed contact with its supporting tree, leaving only a stump of its vine state behind. Its form thickened and lost the pale green color it had shown as the leaves forming the infant basin spouted and began to secrete acid. Tendrils simultaneously rose skyward while its roots poisoned those of its siblings reaching ground too late as well as those of the old core plant. The remainder of the old growth among the trees withered for want of food and water and eventually fell, decayed, and fed the living vegetation of the jungle.

It worked well. Nature had created a viable species and at the same time had seen to it that its very success did not cause it to crowd itself into extinction, a lesson supposedly intelligent humanity would have done well to learn on a great many planets throughout the galaxy in the early days of interstellar exploration.

The price exacted for that balance was another matter. Varn shivered despite the heat. He knew loneliness, isolation from one's own, and he was infinitely glad that this burden had not been laid on his species despite all its acknowledged excesses.

He shook his head to clear it and quickened his pace a little to catch up with his comrades. They were well ahead of him now, and he did not want to lose sight of them. It would be too easy to become lost among these trees.

When he felt comfortable once more, Sogan allowed his pace to slow again. He drew his sleeve across his forehead, then grimaced in disgust. The material was well nigh as wet as

his skin and was considerably dirtier. He would burn everything as soon as they got back to the *Maid* . . .

He reached for his canteen but let it drop back into its sling
untouched. Even with the necessity of replacing the water he
was losing in sweat, some restraint was necessary. It had been
some time now since they had last passed a source of water.
His lips tightened at the memory of that, a wretched little pool
alive with spring leeches.

Would they never leave this hole, he wondered in a
desperation born of revulsion and an exhaustion that was more
than the weariness of muscle. The heat was utterly enervating,
its power trebled by the ceaseless humidity. He felt that if he
did not get some relief from it soon, real relief and not merely
yet another drenching from the rain, he was going to shatter,
either collapse in body or see his nerves, already almost
unbearably taut under the pressure of battling the leeches, snap
completely.

Once more, he drew an arm across his face, and his head
lowered in shame. He was enduring no more than the others.
They were bearing up under it and had a right to expect equal
fortitude from him.

The Arcturian wearily turned his attention back to the hunt
for a signal of their enemies' presence. As always, there was
nothing. The excitement generated by his unit was obvious
enough and clearly illustrated the response he could expect to
find were there other humans in the area, but there was nothing
to match it farther afield. No second party was near their
present position.

He frowned. The blood suckers were everywhere as always,
but the population of the other invisible but normally perceptible creatures seemed strangely low in his immediate
vicinity . . .

His heart gave a painful jolt when he suddenly realized why.
The too-lush moss beneath his feet gave him the answer as
soon as his eyes chanced to drop to it. In his accursed
preoccupation he had strayed into the killing zone of one of the
hunting plants.

He was barely inside, but even as he tensed to spring to
safety, a long green living cord whipped around him, pinning
his arms to his sides and closing so tightly about him that it
drove the breath from his body.

Varn threw his weight against it, struggling to hold his feet, to resist its pull toward the core plant.

That he had to prevent. The thing was immense, eight feet tall or better with a basin of equal proportions. Once he hit the acid it contained, no power of humanity or beyond it would be able to save him.

He was many times heavier than the creatures the tendril normally hunted. He could not free himself, but neither could it draw him in as long as he battled strenuously against it. Hold long enough, a few minutes only, and his comrades would return for him in answer to the call for help his mind even now broadcast . . .

The hunter tightened abruptly with savage force. There was an audible crack, a searing wave of pure agony that seemed to consume all his being, and oblivion slammed in close and tight around him.

TWENTY-FOUR

ISLAEN CONNOR DAMNED herself to several particularly black hells, but even her temper could not keep her mind on the business at hand for long. Fight as she would to concentrate on the work before her, it was becoming increasingly difficult to maintain any kind of satisfactorily consistent search. The heat was draining her mental and physical strength, weakening her power to maintain any sustained effort. They had all been in it too long now, and it was beginning to seriously sap their ability to resist its effects . . .

Fear! The Colonel whirled around. Varn! He was under attack! The assault had come so quickly that he had not been able to set his shields, and she was receiving the full of what he himself was experiencing along with his open call for help.

"A hunter plant's got Varn!" she shouted to the others even as she doubled back along their trail.

The gurry screamed and leaped from her shoulder. "Bandit, stop!" she commanded desperately. "You can't help him this time! You'd only get caught yourself. —Come on back, love," she continued more quietly as Bandit swerved to a stop out of what had been a frantic charge.

The Jadite obeyed, although she remained airborne rather than returning to her former place, knowing battle would be joined soon.

Islaen stumbled and gasped as her consort's sudden pain and loss of consciousness tore into her.

She regained her balance and hurried on, fighting to rein the fear pulsing through her heart and mind. Was it a man she was trying to help or only his now-empty shell?

Sogan had not been traveling far behind his comrades, and the three guerrillas reached the site seconds after their commander had received warning of the attack.

What little color had remained to it drained from the Colonel's face. The battle was over for the Arcturian. He hung limply in the tendril's hold, completely unresisting as it dragged him ever closer to the doom waiting at the plant's immobile heart. Only his size and weight had delayed his end thus far, and his mindless foe was making steady progress despite that difficulty. A few minutes more and it would be over.

The injuries that had so reduced him were readily apparent. Blood stained all his right sleeve, issuing from the gash where the sharp shard of his arm bone had torn through his flesh with such force that it had ripped the sturdy material of both tunic and jacket. The left arm, though the skin was as yet unbroken, was pressed against his body in a manner that told that it, too, was broken. Whether the ribs pinned between them were still sound, she could not immediately tell.

"We'll have to haul him out of there," Jake, who had come to a stop beside her, stated. "You two, burn through that blasted thing and then cover us. There'll be more of them."

The woman nodded briskly. That was the only way to free Varn, and Karmikel alone had the strength to accomplish it quickly enough.

She fired. Her bolt seared through the tendril a foot above the place where it looped around Sogan, severing it. The cut end dropped to the bloodied moss but did not release its hold.

Jake reached the fallen man. The thing was tight as a solar steel rope. He caught hold of it and started to drag the war prince back. Whether he was doing as much harm as good remained to be seen, but he could not delay to arrange a gentler escape. Already, bolts from the women's weapons sliced above his head as they fought to fend off the squad of tendrils dropping from the branches dizzyingly far above.

Even with that screen, he was not sure they would make it. There were so many of the things, and they moved fast . . .

They were free! The Noreenan went a little farther to be certain they were well out of the hunter's range, then he settled Varn as comfortably as he could against a tree.

Islaen went to her knees beside him, her mind penetrating

his body even as she moved. If a knife of bone had slit his lungs, there was probably little they would be able to do for him save to give him as easy a death as they might.

It was long seconds before she withdrew again. She remained still and silent, her head down for a moment while she fought to hold her control. Relief had nearly stripped it from her.

She looked up at last. "He'll be fine. —Help me cut these clothes off. —I'll need water as well and the antibiotics from one of the medical kits." The renewer was already in her hand.

The redheaded Commando-Captain rocked back on his heels, studying Sogan. The ray had done its work. The bones were once more whole, and the tear in his arm was closed, but he was still ghastly pale and showed no sign of regaining consciousness. "He should be coming out of it," he ventured doubtfully.

"Soon," Islaen replied. "Varn's all right now, but the shock of the attack and the pain'll take a while to wear off, and he was as spent as the rest of us before he was ever hit. I'll wake him in a few minutes if he doesn't rouse himself by then, much as I hate to do it."

"Maybe we should just let him be," the demolitions expert said. "He really does look awful, Islaen." That was no understatement. If Sogan were a starship, she would have to declare him derelict-class at the moment.

"I wish we could," her commander answered with a sigh, "but we can't spare the time at this stage, not as long as he can move at all."

The former Admiral woke to find himself pillowed against Islaen. Something restrained his movements. Nets.

He looked around. Their resting place was alive with blood suckers. The repellent was keeping them from actually attacking, but the chemical was not powerful enough to drive them away. His mind lashed out, and he was rewarded by seeing and feeling the squirming obscenities withdraw.

Easy!

He glanced up, smiling at his consort's concern. *I am all right.* He shuddered then and pressed his head against her so that her arms tightened about him in response. *I knew you would come,* he told her with a steadiness that required the command of his will to maintain. *Was it very difficult?*

No, not with the three of us there and well-charged blasters.

He sat up in response to Bandit's excited, relieved whistle and cupped his hand around her.

Their comrades were drawn by her call and were beside the three in the next moment.

"Awake at last?" Jake asked. "How are you doing?"

"Surviving, and glad enough of that. —I owe you again, I suppose?"

The redhead just shrugged. He lifted Sogan's pack and set it nearer to him. "It's lighter now," he informed him. "You'll have to make do with the jacket and tunic you're wearing. We had to burn the others. All that blood was driving the local leeches into a frenzy."

The war prince grimaced. "It will be best to get out of here as soon as we can. They are too interested even yet, despite my transmissions."

"Take your time, Admiral," the other man told him. "I'll cart you on my back if necessary, but I don't find the idea very appealing."

In answer, Varn came to his feet, Islaen and Karmikel steadying him. "I am ready, Comrades, or I will be by the time you three pull on your packs."

TWENTY-FIVE

NOTHING FURTHER HAPPENED to distract or delay them in the hours that followed. The Arcturian kept on with his search, breaking off only when he felt weariness begin to weaken his control and always resuming his hunt after a brief rest had restored him again.

It was to no avail, and in the end, his mind touched Islaen's. *There is nothing, no sign of human intervention whatsoever. Are you certain we are on course?*

Aye. Our information's been dead accurate thus far. She paused. *It's not unreasonable, Varn. These sons don't seem to be invaders. They're just using Amazoon as a convenient place to stash their contraband. They'd have no reason to venture very far from their base.*

I suppose you are right.

The woman studied him closely. He seemed well enough, but she knew how good he could be at concealing discomfort or difficulty.

How's the headache? she asked.

Not bad. I can more or less ignore it, especially when I am concentrating on searching. There was no point in denying a condition she already knew existed. That would serve only to worry the Commando-Colonel.

Here, take a couple more of these. They'll block it for a while.

She frowned when he hesitated. *What's wrong, Varn? They're not addictive, and they have no side effects. Your people don't court needless punishment.*

Sorry, he said quickly, accepting the tablets and swallowing

169

them with a sip of water from his canteen. *I guess I was half off collecting stardust.*

You're just tired. —Let me know if it gets to be too much, she pleaded. *Our repellents will hold us awhile, more than long enough to give you a break.*

Aye, Colonel. I will help no one if I drive myself into the ground. He gave her a wan smile. *You may trust that I do not want to finish this business on Jake's back.*

Sogan retreated behind his shields as soon as the woman returned to her work. No, he thought, Arcturians did not court punishment as a mark of virtue, but he might well have been unconsciously doing so. Some payment should be exacted for entertaining the possibility of defiling himself, of betraying the humanity he had believed basic to himself. There were some fates too vile for any living being, however dark, and to his mind, what he contemplated ranked among these. He could not have faced it . . .

He shook his head as if to clear it. He was too tired to deal with this now. There were too many concrete concerns to claim what remained of his strength. The future and whatever burdens it laid on him would have to see to itself.

Varn felt the flow of power streaming out from Islaen and went back to scanning Amazoon's wildlife, all the while cursing the whole mission for the miserable, ill-favored charter it had proven itself to be. A tremor that he was unable to quell ran through his heart and mind, and he cursed the black-starred assignment again for the utter darkness it could too easily become.

The change happened suddenly but so gently that the war prince nearly missed the outer fringes of it. An eagerness was radiating from the horde of leeches, a patient eagerness that overrode the bitter frustration that accompanied it so closely as to almost seem part of it.

He quickly linked with his consort. Her eyes slitted. *We're on them, I think. Good work, Varn.*

The Colonel tried but could make no contact with any of the other off-worlders. *The blood suckers send out their call over a pretty wide area,* she commented in grudging admiration. *My talent won't take me as far.*

There are a lot more of them, her husband replied, smiling.

He was serious again in the next moment. *They are traveling in response to it. There are few here, and those are on the move. I can feel a concentration ahead of us like the population back in the riverbed and possibly greater.*

Nearly three quarters of an hour passed before Islaen Connor stopped and raised her hand to signal her comrades to keep silent. She was receiving them now, the transmissions of a sizable number of human minds. No particular emotion predominated, just the general hum of life and activity, slightly tinged with relief or some emotion akin to it.

That last did not please the guerrilla leader. There was only one reason for such a feeling in spacers stationed deep in the jungles of Amazoon of Indra. She and her comrades were rapidly running out of time.

She made her report to the others, giving them all the detail she had received or could surmise from the mind patterns.

"Pirates?" Jake asked when she had finished. Although Islaen could not read thought apart from her dealings with Sogan and Bandit, she had long practice in deciphering the emotions she received from others. The minds of the crews manning the wolf packs infesting so many of the ultrasystem's starlanes were marked by such cruelty, violence, and lust for bloodletting that the renegades were usually readily identifiable.

"Some almost certainly are, though I'm not entirely sure about the rest. They're all a bad lot, anyway." Her lips curled in distaste. "Pirates or no, we're dealing with a proper nest of vermin. That much, I can tell you for a fact."

The gurry whistled for attention. *Bandit scout now?*

"Aye," she said. "It's time."

"Keep a fix both on their camp and on us," Sogan instructed. "You will not help us if we have to go looking for you."

Bandit won't get lost! the Jadite declared indignantly.

He chuckled. "I hope you do not. —When you reach the clearing, link both your eyes and ears with mine."

Yes, Varn!

"Remember to warn him first before you do, though," the Colonel cautioned. "Varn won't be at all pleased if you take him by surprise and knock him on his head."

Bandit'll be careful!

"Just see that you are," the former Admiral growled. He glanced at Jake, who was obviously enjoying thoroughly what he heard and could guess of the exchange. He said nothing more. That would only serve to provoke open laughter.

All of them tensed as the little hen vanished from their sight, then started out on their own slower course.

Bandit could fly rapidly when she chose, and such a distance was no problem for a being whose kind had developed following the migrating goldbeast herds on her native Jade. The Federation party had been traveling again for only a short while before Sogan's head snapped up. Karmikel quickly lay a hand on his shoulder, knowing Bandit would not give him much time before claiming control of his senses.

There was the usual dizzy riot of impressions, then Varn regained command over the images pouring into his mind.

He was looking down upon a very large clearing cradled on one side by a bend of the Matron and walled in by the jungle on every other. It was surrounded by an extremely tight energy picket that bent inward at its top to form a roof over the whole complex.

Sogan strained to peer through the brilliant screen. Bandit swooped low over it, keeping just enough above it to avoid any chance of brushing against it.

He could see then, well enough to make out the detail he needed.

The whole clearing had been burned clean of vegetation. Two large quan huts were set up in the shade afforded by the branches of the great trees reaching over the open area. Warehouses. Munitions were always sensitive, and no master kept them aboard any longer than necessary to actually transport them. The crews would be following usual spacer custom and bunking on their vessels.

The starships were there. Three were precisely what the Amazoonan report indicated, ten-man freighters, fast, well-maintained craft whose skins were sound but told of much hard use over a long span of time. He could guess the nature of their crews readily enough given the impressions Islaen had received from them—smugglers of the type who sought out charters most of their kind would not touch, vermin scarcely above pirates and earning the same penalty when they were taken with some of their vile cargoes.

There was a fourth vessel far bigger than the others, a small brig, thirty-class. Her hull was the gleaming silver of a ship that enjoyed steady on-world maintenance.

The hands were stripped to the waist, or waist and halter in the case of the women, their trouser legs cut off at midthigh, sure proof of the effectiveness of their picket. The small insects penetrating it were not numerous enough to force them to cover up in defense even if they had no repellent to hold them at bay.

It was a busy scene. The crews of all four vessels were sweating and cursing as they lugged material from the quan huts to the brig. Even from his high vantage, he could make out the Navy markings on the crates. There were larger items as well, long cylinders as deadly as they looked—surplanetary and space-to-atmosphere missiles.

The war prince watched the loading a short while longer, then he quietly withdrew and reactivated his own sense receptors.

He was not long in describing what he had seen. A gloomy silence followed his account.

At last, Jake Karmikel shook his head. "It's over, then. We're too late. That brig'll be off-world before nightfall. We haven't a hope of getting a crack at her."

Varn Tarl Sogan's eyes dropped, then raised once more. His expression was as tight as the shields he had set about his thoughts. This was it, the fulfillment of his premonition that he would lose more on Amazoon of Indra than the life he would soon no longer value, or it would be if any part at all of what he intended to do went sour. "Those arms do not have to be blown," he said quietly. "We need only prevent that vermin from taking them."

"Right!" the redhead agreed sarcastically. "Now, how do you propose . . ."

Islaen's nails dug into Karmikel's arm, silencing him. Her eyes were on Sogan. His face was white and set, determined. His eyes gazed beyond them into some hell of his own. It was a look she had seen on him before, when she had watched him from the spy post to his private quarters on Thorne of Brandine on the day he had chosen to burn his commander's order, sparing the planet and working his own ruin. —Spirit of Space! What was he thinking now?

The Arcturian continued as if he had not heard Jake. "We shall have to get that energy picket down," he said, "preferably all of it simultaneously and with delayed action charges so that we can regroup before they go off."

"No problem at all, Admiral," the demolitions expert told him, "provided we get there before they lift, and from what you've told us, we should be able to manage that with time to spare."

TWENTY-SIX

THE FEDERATION PARTY had an hour of hard, fast walking before they came on the clearing Varn had observed through Bandit's eyes. The work had progressed rapidly in the interim, and only a few of the heaviest crates remained to be put aboard the big ship.

The gurry flew down to them from her perch in the canopy, where she had remained on watch to give the unit warning of any drastic change in the activity below her.

Moving quickly and in total silence, the four Commandos crept along the perimeter of the picket, setting the charges Bethe Danlo had prepared before they began their last march for the camp, Islaen and Jake taking the most exposed stretches.

That along the bank of the river was extremely open, and the Colonel pressed herself to the ground, using every shadow of cover available to her. Fortunately, the renegades had not bothered with the area outside their picket once they had established their camp, and the weeds that had claimed the burned-over place were thick and high. Only the patch they used to reach the water was still clear and bare, but that was at the farther end, and she would not have to cross it.

Her progress was slow and infinitely careful. She knew the others would be finished well ahead of her, but that could not be helped. Set this growth moving, and she would betray herself, betray them all.

At last, she was done. The Noreenan retraced her route with the same painful caution until she gained the shelter of the jungle once more. After that, she quickly made her way to the place she had designated as their rendezvous. As she had anticipated, the rest of her team were waiting for her there.

Islaen's arrival marked the end of their preparations and the beginning of Varn Tarl Sogan's ordeal. His comrades turned curious eyes on the former Admiral. Thus far, they had followed his orders on trust, but he would now have to reveal his plan.

Sogan lay flat beside Islaen. He rested his forehead on his arm. He did not want to look at any of them. Any failure whatsoever on his part, and he would be a pariah in their eyes. A major flaw in either his plan or his execution of it would mean their deaths.

"Keep your blasters at ready," he whispered. "We will need them if I cannot protect us."

The Commando-Colonel looked sharply at him, realizing at last what he intended to do. Fortunately, their comrades did not yet know. Not that they would give him any argument if they did. This was the only way they had of holding those arms on Amazoon of Indra.

She could feel the power flowing out from the war prince, some of it shielding them, reinforcing the commands he had been broadcasting since they had discovered he could master Amazoon's leeches, the rest calling . . .

The whole perimeter of the camp erupted in light and noise as the guerrillas' charges detonated almost in a single blast. When peace returned in the next moment, the deadly energy barrier was gone.

All inside was a mass of confusion; the spacers were shouting to one another, diving for the almost nonexistent cover they had left, drawing the arms they had not needed on Amazoon until this moment.

Varn Tarl Sogan paid them no heed. His mind lashed out, filled with the images of blazing brush and burning nests and with dark pictures of those who had set the fires.

Other things needed no such encouragement to attack . . .

Bandit made no sound, but she flew at the Arcturian, tearing at his head and neck with her claws. *Varn, stop! Bad! Bad!*

Be quiet! Islaen Connor commanded as sharply as she had ever spoken to the gurry. *Go to Jake, and don't interfere again!*

She shuddered in her own heart, but the guerrilla leader linked her mind with her husband's, strengthening his efforts.

He needed help, and the Jadite would give him none, not with this.

The crown wasps had already massed at Sogan's call, his warning of danger to their kind, which he had been broadcasting ever since he had known what his course must be. They responded now in their thousands and hundred thousands.

The collective swarm hit the clearing in one great wave, a wave that did not ebb but only continued to swell as the warriors and workers of still other nests arrived to augment it.

Amazoon's leeches came with them, not in answer to the war prince's summons but in response to their own instinct as the way to their eagerly coveted prey opened before them. Their bodies pulsed and looped along the ground until the brown soil was covered by a glistening, dark silver layer that advanced with terrifying speed.

Varn fought them, fought with all the strength within him. The wasps were one thing, no worse in their way than the lasers and missiles of a conventional military attack. The blood suckers were something else. Renegades or no, this was a horror nothing human, nothing living, should have to endure, or could be permitted to endure. The responsibility was his and the responsibility to prevent what was and could only be judged an atrocity the equal of anything the worst of his kind had perpetrated in the bitter course of the War. Only he was capable of stopping it.

Sogan battled the ravenous horde with every command, every image he had learned could influence them, bending all the force of his will in a massive effort to recall them, to dam their charge.

There was no halting them! There were too many, and they were too excited. Some had already attached themselves and begun feeding, and their transmissions coupled with the scent of the blood drawn by the crown wasps' stingers gave the lie to the commands and the suggestions he was trying to implant.

Desperately, the man threw more and more of his strength into his fight, drew ever deeper from himself until he reached the core of his being, the energy supporting his own life, even as he had done on Jade of Kuan Yin and Omrai of Umbar.

Searing pain exploded within him, ripping through his head, his mind.

It was only a warning. He realized that even as it struck, and he tried to grip himself to continue the battle, but his hold on consciousness was wavering . . .

Islaen Connor's strength poured into him, supporting him until he could stabilize himself once more.

She resisted when he sought to draw on her power to more directly fuel his effort. *It's lost, Varn*, she said sharply. *Pull out. —You have no choice, man! If you die now or destroy your mind, we're all dead. They're already coming for us.*

He saw at once that she was right. Some of the blood suckers were moving away from the clearing, heading for the place where they were lying with an eagerness that sickened him to his soul. He dared spare no more of his strength in what he should have known from the start was a futile attempt. The shields protecting his own party were too near breaking under the excitement firing the blood suckers.

Shuddering in heart and body, he broke off his effort to screen his enemies from this ghastly adjunct to his attack. Those who reached the Matron would live. With luck, that would be most of them. The rest . . . Many might have survived the crown wasps. None would be left after the leeches. Living and wasp-slain alike would be bled dry, probably within a matter of minutes.

It did not take long for the spacers to shatter utterly. Some raced for the nonexistent shelter of their open starships or the quan huts, staggering under a living cloud of the fiercely stinging wasps, their legs coated with greedily drinking, rapidly expanding leeches. The most made for the river, and those first reaching it cast themselves into its shielding embrace.

The water churned into a froth even as they struck it. There were screams, a few, and those short-lived, as the foam turned scarlet.

Varn stiffened, but there was no other break in the masklike calm he had clamped over himself. Even in this, he was thwarted. He knew the wild hunger radiating from out of the boiling river. There was no escape for him, no more than there was for his victims. The deed was his, the whole of it, and he was fated to carry its full weight.

The off-worlders still heading for the Matron faltered, seeing what had happened to their faster comrades, but they were maddened by the wasps and by the leeches clamped to their feet and lower legs, and the better part of them went on, preferring the jaws of those things waiting for them in the water to the slower agony of the deaths they would as surely meet on land. Only the very few who had not dropped their blasters in the nightmare of the crown wasps' initial assault were able to free themselves mercifully from where they stood.

Within ten minutes, it was over. The wasps lifted from the clearing where nothing human remained alive, leaving what was left on land to the suckers of those leeches fortunate enough to find a place to fix themselves on one of the corpses. The swarms, spent with the fury of their attack, did not trouble them in their feasting.

There was no budging the feeding blood suckers, nor would there be until they had drunk their fill, but as the excitement and hope faded in the vastly greater number of the creatures disappointed of a meal, Sogan was gradually able to dismiss them, to send them back into the treelands whence they had come.

Only when the ground was once more clear did he come to his feet, a signal that freed his comrades as well.

"You bastard," Jake Karmikel hissed. "You Arcturian bastard."

The gurry hissed as well, a sharp, penetrating sound unpleasant and slightly painful to human ears. *Jake's right! Varn did very bad! Islaen, too!* She took wing, not flying to any of the Commandos but soaring up into the canopy far overhead.

Varn looked from one to the other of them. He did not speak but lowered his head, as if in acquiescence, and, his mind completely sealed, turned and walked into the jungle, away from the clearing and from his comrades.

Bethe Danlo was the first to rouse from the shock of the horror they had just witnessed. She whirled on her husband, her eyes blazing like a pair of exploding stars in her fury. "You hard-finned, hypocritical son of a Scythian ape!" she snarled. "How dare you condemn him? We couldn't have done what he did, and we didn't realize what he planned to do, but we should have known what would happen as soon as the picket came down, and we saw what he was about fast enough once he'd started. We could've stopped him, Jake Karmikel, any one of us could've, just by breaking his concentration before he got those things really going. We damned well didn't even try. By my lights, that makes us just as responsible as he is, every one of us except Bandit. She did make the attempt."

She pulled herself under control. "You said you owed him. Now get off your fins and repay some atom of that debt. You blasted him. You have to be the one to go after him."

Fear suddenly tightened her voice. "Move, damn you! How much time do you think he's going to give us after this?"

Karmikel ran. Bethe had been right in reaming him and right in her assessment of what the former Admiral would do. Whatever the means he had used to complete their mission, he did not want to see Varn Tarl Sogan dead, by his own hand or by any other's.

The war prince had gone a good distance from his companions before stopping and was just drawing his blaster when Jake reached him.

The Noreenan's hand slammed down on his, forcing the weapon back into its holster. "No more of that rot! You're in the Federation now, not the Empire."

"This is still my right . . ."

"If you were a civilian, aye, but you're Navy, and you've got a mission to complete. We're not out of this yet. We have to check out the camp. That's going to be a real joy, especially combing those ships and quan huts. It might be nice to spare Islaen and Bethe some of it." He eyed the other coldly. "Besides, the two of us'd have a plaguey hard time trying to do it all by ourselves."

That reached him, as he had intended. "Two?"

"You put that thing to your head now, and what do you think Islaen Connor will do? If I'm not greatly mistaken, she helped you. Bandit wouldn't, judging from the way she attacked you, and you couldn't have managed it all alone. If you're condemned, where does that leave her?"

The former Admiral's eyes flashed. "There's no guilt on her!"

"No," he replied gently, "and none on you, either, my friend. —I was navigating off the charts back there. None of us liked what happened, but it'd have been a galaxy worse to let those arms escape to be turned loose on some innocent populace."

Sogan made him no answer, but he turned back toward the ravaged clearing. Jake felt the tension melt from him. The problem might not be solved long-term, but the Arcturian would not try this again until they were back at the Navy base on Horus, well away from Amazoon of Indra. Hopefully, they would be able to come up with some more effective way to deal with it by then.

TWENTY-SEVEN

JAKE KARMIKEL CLIMBED the core ladder connecting the various levels of the *Fairest Maid* until he reached the deck he wanted. He swung off there and went into a small crew's cabin, that in which the starship's personnel and passengers spent the bulk of their off-duty waking time. Bethe and Islaen were there along with a patently miserable Bandit, but there was no sign of the war prince.

"Still on the bridge?" he asked.

"Aye," replied the Colonel. "He's been shut up there ever since we planeted."

"He's all right?" he asked sharply.

"Just wonderful," the woman replied bitterly. "He hasn't tried to use a blaster on himself again. Yet. I won't have to worry about that until we've been formally debriefed."

"Will he do it?"

"Who knows? You handled him pretty well by drawing me into it, but I haven't a clue as to what he's thinking. He won't let anyone near him, physically or in mind, not even Bandit."

"This is a good part my fault," Karmikel said glumly after a brief pause. "It may have worked for the time being, but I should never have mentioned your sharing responsibility for any of it. That had to just about double his guilt load."

"Now don't you start with that debris! I have more than enough of it with him!"

"Sorry, lass." He sighed. "I just wish he were the kind of man I could take out and get good and drunk."

"I know, Jake, but it wouldn't help anyway. It was an atrocity in point of fact, a particularly gruesome one, whatever the nature of the victims. There's no getting around that, even if he did not intend for it to go so far."

Her head lowered. "I can't blame him, I suppose. He never tolerated butcher work during the War and paid heavily because he wouldn't engage in it, and now . . ." Her eyes closed. "The Spirit of Space forgive me! Why didn't I pull out of it faster back there? I'd known he didn't want a total massacre, and I knew he couldn't stop it once it had begun. He never called those damned blood suckers, and he nearly killed himself trying to drive them off. As for the sawmills, they were as big a surprise to him . . ."

"Nothing would've been fast enough!" the Sergeant interjected sharply. "It was a call to duty and to your aid that stopped him then, not any comfort or support that we could offer. What matters now is what you're going to do."

The Colonel smiled tightly. "Go back to work. We all need another mission to wash the taste of this last one out of our mouths. I've already put in the request."

Karmikel's eyes darkened. "I hate sounding like a proper bastard, but can Sogan pull it feeling the way he is? I don't want to get killed because he can't."

"You have no fear of that with Varn Tarl Sogan," his commander responded icily.

She came to her feet. "It's time I told him what I've done," she said decisively.

The other two rose as well. Both knew the challenge Islaen was about to face and that it was one she had to tackle alone.

"We'll be on the *Jovian Moon*," Jake said. "Let us know when you have the details."

"Will do, Comrade. Thanks."

Islaen Connor paused at the door to the bridge. Her heart was beating fast. She had been playing the coward, but this could be put off no longer. It was just that she realized so well that any mishandling on her part would probably be fatal . . .

She touched Bandit. She had hesitated about allowing the gurry to accompany her, but she might help, and the Jadite was sensitive enough to withdraw if her two humans needed to be alone.

She knocked. Mental speech was useless with the Arcturi-

an's shields set so tightly against her, and so she called aloud,
"I have to talk to you, Varn. Let me in."

"The door is open, Colonel."

Sogan was sitting back in his flight chair, looking out
through the observation panels at the activity in the Navy's
portion of Horus' huge spaceport. He nodded in greeting to
her, but there was no light or life in his eyes.

Determination firmed in her. "Varn, please. This has to
stop," the woman told him as she sat on the arm of his chair.
"You're breaking Bandit's heart. You're not doing me any
good, either, but I can at least get mad at you. She can't.
Feeling's too direct with her."

"You are angry now?"

"I should be, but I only wish I could heal you."

His eyes closed. "Not even you can do that. I did this to
myself."

"Did you? Really?"

He turned away. "I sullied myself irrevocably, and I sullied
you."

"Rot! I helped you of my own free will because it was
something that had to be done. —You intended that those
renegades should have the river for a refuge until you could
finally calm the wildlife down and send them on their way. You
had no idea that the sawmills were in that stretch of water."

"I should have checked . . ." A shudder ran through his
body. "I knew the leeches were there, but I believed I could
handle them."

Aye, she thought. That part of it was riding him worse than
any of the rest. He had so detested the blood suckers
himself . . . "What choice did you have?" she countered.
"Besides, those spacers were real vermin. From the identifi-
cations we've made already, what happened was barely adequate justice for the most of them. The same couldn't be said
for the people the arms would've finished off or enslaved had
they gotten away."

"I know all that!" His eyes fell. "It-does not alter what
happened, not for me."

Islaen said nothing for a moment. Varn did not enjoy
killing—his heroism citation had been won for risking his own
life in defense of others, not for taking lives, although many a
renegade had died through his efforts—and this had been so

grim. "We weren't much help to you, any of us," she said, once more bitterly aware of her own failure.

Bandit was perched beside him and now whimpered. He could not bear her pain and reached out to comfort her. Her answering purr was pitiful in its eagerness.

"None of this is your fault, Little Bandit," he told her quietly. "You were the strongest of us and the best. You cannot be expected to understand that good humans must sometimes do very bad things to prevent worse evil still."

Varn meant less hurt!

"Aye, small one, but intention cannot always be fulfilled, either."

"You've just argued your own case," Islaen Connor said softly.

"Logically." He groped for words. "I cannot make it mean anything. —The mission was sour from the start . . ." His head lowered. "I wish I knew what to do, Islaen."

"Do you want to leave the Navy?"

He hesitated, and fear gripped her heart. If he ran now, he was finished, as a man, even if he chose to keep his blaster holstered.

"No. —I just need time to think, to work this out for myself, though I have been making a poor enough job of that thus far."

Her eyes shadowed. "I've done wrong, then. I asked Admiral Sithe for another mission."

He looked at her sharply. "You have seen him already?"

"Just briefly."

"What did you tell him?" he asked carefully.

"That Amazoon's wildlife beat us to it on this one and apologized that they did so thorough a job, depriving us of potential witnesses." Her brows raised. "You didn't think I'd mention our talents, did you?"

"No, naturally not." He felt relieved, however, and gave her the ghost of a smile.

It faded in the next moment, but the Arcturian compelled his mind to turn from his own misery. As long as he was part of this unit, it was his to conduct himself accordingly. Wounds, physical or to the spirit, must await their appropriate time and turn for attention. "This new mission, have you any information on it yet?"

"Not enough to give us a start." Her head raised. "I told

Ram Sithe that we wanted to see this out, to be the ones to take the buyer and/or mastermind of that arms grab."

Sogan sat bolt upright. "You what?"

Her eyes flashed. "I want vengeance as I have never wanted it before in all my life," she said savagely. "We five are bound by more than convenience and Navy order, Varn Tarl Sogan. What happened on Amazoon of Indra happened to every one of us, and the source of it, the ultimate cause of it all, is the greed and lust for power of one person or group of people. I want them dead by my blaster or locked in a Federation pen for the remainder of their natural lives."

The Colonel drew a deep breath to quiet the emotion gripping her. "Such subbiotics remain a threat as long as their fangs are unpulled. In this case, I think we've more than earned the right to do the yanking."

His own head lifted. Islaen was correct. Their entire unit had been violated in this, not just him, although he was the focus of what had occurred. None of them would be truly cleansed until they brought the case to a full close, and it was his business above any of the others' to see it completed, completed to their full satisfaction.

What he had lost could not be restored. Only revenge, payment, could be sought. The stain to his honor could not be erased.

That was his concern. His duty to the others must take precedence over it. "We have that right, Islaen Connor," he replied steadily.

His dark eyes studied her. She was tired, he saw, spent with her efforts on Amazoon and with worry. "We have earned the right to some peace as well," he said more gently, "and I vow on my soul that we shall have a share of that soon, after our work on this is done."

He held out his hand to her, closing her fingers between his as his mind suddenly opened to hers. *We have a big task before us, my Islaen. It is time we bent ourselves to it.*